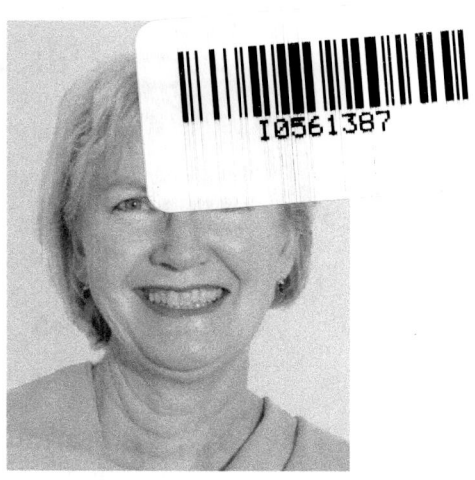

Karen grew up in a small country town in north-eastern Victoria, Australia. She spent her childhood riding horses through beautiful scenery of eucalypts, lakes, and snow-capped mountains and her love of landscape deeply affects her writing. She worked in a range of educational settings and holds a Ph.D. and M.Ed. (Hons) in the areas of fantasy. She is particularly interested in the power of the hero's inner journey which she explores through Deep Fantasy. Karen has travelled extensively overseas but enjoys nothing more than camping in the Australian Outback. She lives in Melbourne and now writes full-time. You can find out more about Karen and her books on her website.

Connect with K. S. Nikakis

Amazon: https://www.amazon.com/author/ksnikakis
Twitter: https://twitter.com/KSNikakis
Facebook: www.facebook.com/ksnikakis
Goodreads: www.goodreads.com
Website: www.ksnikakis.com
Email: author@ksnikakis.com

WORKS BY K S NIKAKIS

Non Fiction

Journey: Seeking the Sacred, Spirit and Soul in the Australian Wilderness

Fantasy Novels
Series

Angel Caste series:
Angel Blood
Angel Breath
Angel Bone
Angel Bound
Angel Blessed
Angel Caste – Complete 5 Book Series

The Kira Chronicles trilogy:*
The Whisper of Leaves
The Song of the Silvercades
The Cry of the Marwing
remnant hard copies only

The Kira Chronicles series:
The Whisper of Leaves
The Silence of Stone
The Secrets of Stars
The Thunder of Hoofs
The Crying of Birds
The Music of Home
The Kira Chronicles – Complete 6 Book Series

Fantasy Novels

The Emerald Serpent
Heart Hunter
The Third Moon
Messenger
I Heard the Wolf Call My Name – *Finalist - Best YA*
Novel Aurealis Awards, 2019

Fantasy Short Stories

The Gift
The Tale of Prince Anura
Dragon Sprite
Glass-Heart – *Finalist – Best YA*
Short Story Aurealis Awards, 2019

THE SILENCE OF STONE

K.S. NIKAKIS

First published by SOV CONSULTING LLC - SOV
Media Australia 2018
Amazon: www.amazon.com.au

Publisher: SOV CONSULTING LLC - SOV Media
Melbourne, Australia.

Cover by AS Nikakis: http://asnikakis.com
Shutterstock.com/nutriaaa

National Library of Australia
Cataloguing-in-Publication entry:
Nikakis, Karen Simpson
The Silence of Stone Book 2 The Kira Chronicles Series
ISBN 978-0-6482652-8-3

For Con, Chrysanthe and Andreas

THE SILENCE OF STONE

MAP OF ALLOGRENIA

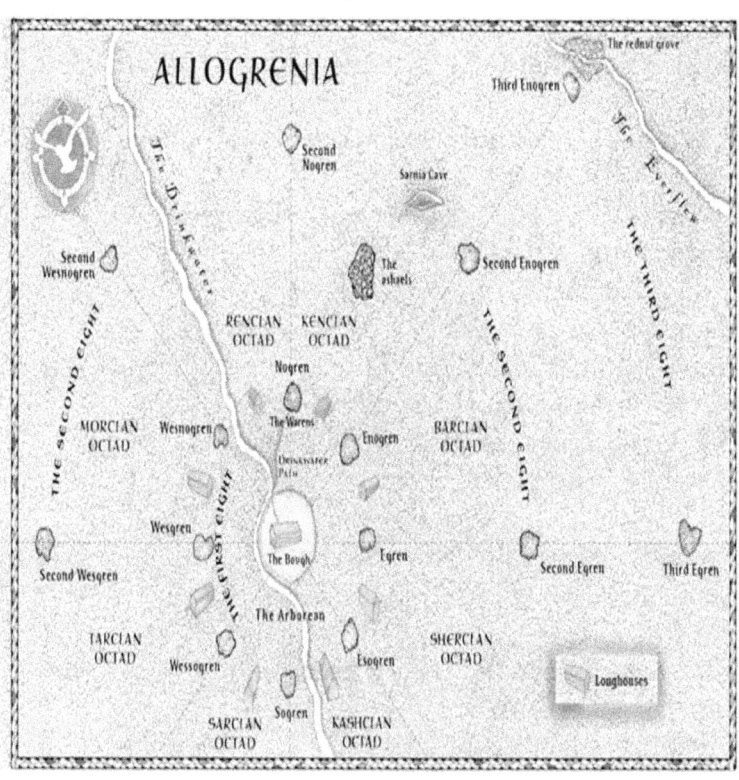

The Tremen

Of the Bough – Tremen heart of healing
Maxen (dec) – Kashclan - Tremen Leader
Fasarini (dec) – Sarclan – bondmate of Maxen
Merek (dec) – eldest son of Maxen
Lern (dec) – second eldest son of Maxen
Kiraon (Kira) – daughter of Maxen
Kandor (dec) – youngest son of Maxen
Sendra (dec) (helper) – Sarclan

Kashclan – descended from Kasheron
Miken – Clanleader
Tenerini – Barclan – bondmate of Miken
Tresen – son of Miken
Mikini – daughter of Miken
Brem – experienced Healer and Protector
Arlen – learner Healer and Protector
Paterek – learner Healer and Protector
Werem – learner Healer and Protector
Kertash – Protector Leader

Sarclan – descended from Sarkash
Berendash – Clanleader

Tarclan – descended from Taren
Farish – (dec) Clanleader
Kemrick - Clanleader
Sarkash – (dec) Protector Commander

Morclan – descended from Mormesh
Marren – Clanleader
Kest – Protector Commander
Kesilini – sister of Kest
Feseren – (dec) Protector
Misilini – Barclan – bondmate of Feseren
Penedrin – Protector

Renclan – descended from Renen
Sanden – Clanleader
Pekrash – Protector Leader
Sanaken – (dec) Protector

Kenclan – descended from Kentash
Tenedren – Clanleader
Senden – Protector Leader

Barclan – descended from Baren
Ketten – Clanleader

Sherclan – descended from Sheren
Dakresh – Clanleader
Sener – elder son of Dakresh
Bern – younger son of Dakresh
Bendrash – Protector Leader

The Shargh

Erboran – (dec) Chief
Arkendrin – younger brother of Erboran
Ergardrin (dec) – father of Erboran and Arkendrin
Tarkenda – join-wife of Ergardrin - mother of Erboran and Arkendrin
Palansa – join-wife of Erboran – Chief-wife – guardian of next Chief

Loyal to Erboran
Erdosin
Irsulalin
Ormadon
Erlken
Irmakin
and their blood-ties

Loyal to Arkendrin
Irason
Ermashin
Urpalin
Orthaken
Irdodun
Urgundin (dec)
and their blood-ties

Founders of the Four Shargh Peoples
The Shargh – Artmenton
The Soushargh – Urchelen
The Weshargh – Irkardin
The Ashmiri - Ashmiridin

The Silence of Stone

Thus spoke the Last of the Shargh Tellers:

*If Healer sees a setting sun
and gold meets gold, two halves are one,
then Westerner with silver tongue
will love and lose the golden one,
but bind a friendship slow begun.
If horses graze in forests deep
where trees their summer greening keep
then fire will be the flatswords' bane
and bring the dead to life again.
Deeds long past will hunt the Shargh
and funeral smoke consume the stars
until the thing that draws no breath,
devours the dark that feeds on death.*

1

Kira stared at the dull wink of crystal in the stone. Stone floor, stone ceiling, stone walls: the crystal was the only thing to alleviate the bleakness of her surroundings. The stone was dark, not like the pale stone of the Sarnia caves.

She flinched as memories of Feseren's death flooded back and struggled to think of something else, but the caves' name had roused thoughts of the Terak Kutan's stone city too. Kasheron had fled its violence, and now its violence had followed them here.

She sat up and pushed the hair from her eyes. The stone was hard and unforgiving through the mattress. It was the type used by Protectors, thin and stuffed with sere grass that poked at her no matter which way she turned. At least the air carried the spice of morning-bright, not the stone's dank scent. It drifted in from the training room beyond, the Haelen, where the wounded lay.

Tresen had secured cloth across the alcove to give her privacy and a place to sleep, but there was no sleep to be had. Jarin and Marakin's groans were audible, and now she wasn't taken up with healing, her mind filled with visions of Kandor at Turning, leaning out of the Bough's window as he begged her to take him with her. Her throat contracted, and she clutched at the images of falzon bandages being used to bind a wound, to stop the pictures of death and fire before they took hold.

It was almost habit now, this cutting off of memory; a reflexive response to something that had the power to destroy her. If only the same mental sleight of hand could

6

be used to deal with what was to come. Everest still held the most severely wounded but those with lesser wounds already burned. Soon their breathing would mimic Feseren's and like his, each of their rattling gasps would be a testament to her failure.

She hugged herself and as the sleeping-gown slipped low, wrenched it back over her shoulder. It was too big but at least it was clean, and she wondered vaguely who owned it. Certainly not to her: everything of hers had been burned in the Bough. She screwed her eyes shut and visualized the falzon bandage again, then forced her aching bones up from the mattress and paced.

There *must* be a cure for Shargh wounds, the rhyme proved it! *Fire with flatswords brings the bane.* Fire referred to fever; Feseren's death had taught her that. He had burned as those beyond the hanging now burned. *Fire without brings life again.* But fire without *what*? It made no sense! She rubbed at her gritty eyes. How could fever bring life? Fever burned the flesh as surely as flames had burned the Bough. There must be something else!

But what? Where? Two steps to the wall, two back to the mattress. Kasheron's people must have suffered Shargh wounds and the rhyme told her they had survived. The cure hadn't been in the Herbal Sheaf or in the Warens' Writings, moldy or otherwise, *or* in the caverns she had explored so far. And it certainly was not *here*! *If* it had been recorded, it must be deeper in the Warens.

She wrenched off the gown and pulled on the dirty Protector garb that had replaced her finery of Turning. Then she grabbed her pack and peered furtively around the hanging. Tresen was at the far end of the training room bent over a thrashing Protector, which was just as well. She did not have time to argue with him over her safety.

7

She went swiftly through the rows of wounded, snatched up one of the tunnel lamps, and set off into the darkness.

Miken edged round Nogren's trunk into the Warens' outer cavern and nodded to the Protector who sprang from the shadows. It was Darmanin of Kenclan, one of Kest's men. They were all Kest's men now, he corrected, as he strode along the tunnel, and it was fitting. Kest was a strong fighter with a good strategic brain, but more importantly, he had the men's trust. It only remained for the Clancouncil to confirm him as the new Protector Commander.

The air grew danker as he hastened on and his nose wrinkled. The ventilation was better in the training rooms, but it was no place for the ill. Still, they could not risk moving them. The bees-comb of tunnels also kept Kira safe, which was the main thing.

A staccato of footsteps filled the cavern ahead and as the bobbing glow of lamps appeared, Miken flattened himself against the wall. It was a patrol heading out into the trees and their leader shouted orders in preparation for Nogren's passing. Miken stiffened. 'Commander Kest!' He had to bawl, to be heard above the noise of their passing.

The patrol came to a halt and a lamp was passed along the group. 'Clanleader Miken, what brings you to the Warens?' asked Kest. The lamp made his hair as bright as candle-flame, but his blue eyes remained dark.

'I come to speak with Healer Kiraon,' said Miken. His words carried to the back of the patrol and there was a restless movement of feet and a soft mutter.

'I might come with you, Clanleader,' said Kest slowly.

'By all means.'

Kest called one of his men forward and they conferred briefly, and then orders were shouted and the patrol marched on. 'I'm calling a Clancouncil for the morrow,' said Miken, as they walked on together. 'The Clanleaders will formalize your command and appoint Kira Tremen Leader.'

'Do you think it is wise to do that so quickly?'

'What? Appoint you or her?' asked Miken dryly. 'Kira's our best Healer,' he added, when Kest failed to respond.

'I don't doubt Kira's healing skill, but she is still very young and lacks the ability to think before she acts. I . . .' Kest stopped. 'I beg your pardon, Clanleader, I intended no clan insult.'

'I think you and I can dispense with clan niceties in the interests of honesty,' said Miken. 'Kira's lacked a loving hand of guidance and, as you have no doubt noticed, is inclined to go her own way. But the gift of healing is strong in her as is the passion for it that true Healers possess. As for the rest of it . . .' Miken shrugged. 'It will come with time.'

Kest wondered whether she would be given that time, but he said nothing and, for a while the only sound was the grit of their boots over the cavern floor. It was Miken who broke the silence. 'Has she spoken of Kandor?'

'I have had little time to visit the training rooms,' said Kest, 'but Protector Tresen reports that she calls his name in nightmare. She hasn't grieved openly for him though, nor spoken of anything that happened that night, and he daren't raise it with her.'

'Kira had great love for Kandor. She . . .' Miken's voice cracked, and he slammed his hand into the stone.

'He was only a boy yet the stinking murderers ignored Protectors to kill him!'

Kest waited for Miken's breathing to quieten. 'Since we last met, I've received the reports of the Protectors who fought that night.'

Miken's head flicked round. 'And?'

'The Shargh left their dead where they fell, all except one.'

'They took a body back?'

'Yes.'

'You think it was their leader?'

'Who else? No others were accorded the privilege.' There was a brief silence while Miken digested the news. 'I've also been thinking about the manner of their attack,' continued Kest. 'They passed Barclan and Kenclan longhouses to reach the Bough, making it a journey of over four days from the Sentinels. If they were simply intent on killing Tremen, they could have sated their appetites earlier and with far less trouble. Clanleaders Tenedren and Ketten had set no guards.'

'I've had the same thought,' said Miken. 'Go on.'

'Then there's the first attack. They choked Kandor unconscious, but they clearly intended to kill Kira.'

'What are you saying?'

'Why didn't they kill Kandor then? A hand over his mouth and a sword across his throat. It would have been easy, and then when Kira came to his aid, kill her too.'

Miken's blood ran cold. Kest's words held a terrible logic. 'You think they had no real interest in killing Kandor because they hunted Kira? And that, having failed to kill her then, they came to the Bough for her, and ignored the longhouses along the way?'

'Yes.'

10

'I don't suppose you've thought of any reasons why they might hunt her?' Kest shrugged, his discomfited face clear in the wash of light from the cavern-turned Haelen ahead. 'Have you spoken of this to others?'

Kest shook his head. 'To be honest, now I've voiced my thoughts aloud, they seem improbable.'

'It's best they remain between us for the time being,' said Miken softly, his gaze on the cavern they neared, 'and that Kira remains in the Warens until the Shargh's intentions are clearer.' The Haelen had changed little since Kest's last visit. The wounded still lay in neat rows and the air still held the scent of morning-bright. It reminded him of Misilini's birthing-room, and of how he had scooped Kira from the floor after she had brought Feseren's son safely into the world. There was no sign of Kira though, just Tresen at the far end of the cavern, bent in tending.

He rose at their approach and bowed to Kest, before Miken embraced him. The attack had left them all with a keener appreciation of those they loved, conceded Kest. His eyes swept the room and he tensed as he took in Kesilini's empty mattress. There were two other mattresses with their covers folded neatly on top too.

'Kesilini is helping Arlen prepare herbs in the last training room,' said Tresen, seeing his gaze, 'and we have had two deaths.'

'Who?' asked Miken sharply.

'Renclansman Marakin and Tarclansman Jarin.'

'But they weren't badly wounded,' exclaimed Kest.

'No. They only had need of sickleseed, not everest, but we've since discovered everest staves off the rot longer,' said Tresen.

'Then give them all everest,' said Kest.

'There's always a risk with everest the sleeper won't wake,' said Miken.

'And in the end, everest only postpones the rot, not destroys it,' added Tresen grimly.

'Where's Kira?' asked Miken.

'Sleeping,' said Tresen, and nodded towards the far end of the cavern. 'She refused to leave the wounded so I set up a bed for her here. It's the first real rest she's had since this started.'

'I might just check,' said Miken, and moved off.

'How is she, Tresen?' asked Kest softly, his gaze on Miken's retreating back.

'The same. She does what she must for the injured, but barely speaks *or* eats. Kesilini has worked with her today.'

Kest's eyebrows rose. 'Kesilini?'

'Kesilini's idea not mine,' said Tresen with a smile. 'I suggested she be escorted back to your longhouse, but she reminded me she was Kira's bond-sister. I hoped Kesilini's grief might help Kira with hers, but I don't think it has. Kira loved Kandor more than anything in the world.' Tresen's voice cracked and he clenched his jaw.

And you loved him too, thought Kest. He remembered how, as a young Protector, he had seen Kira, Tresen, and Kandor at play amongst the trees. He had not known who they were then; they had just been three Kashclan children but always together. And now, Kandor was dead and, in a round-about way, Tresen had reminded him that Kira was his bond-sister.

There was a stifled exclamation and Kest turned to see Miken hastening back through the wounded, clearly upset. 'Kira's not there!'

'She must be!' said Tresen in alarm. 'She said she was going to sleep.'

'Is there anywhere else she could be?' asked Kest, more calmly than he felt.

'The Herbery in the last training room, or the latrines, but if she'd gone to either place, she wouldn't have . . .' Tresen stopped.

'Sneaked out while your back was turned?' finished Kest. 'Well, the entrances to the Warens are guarded, so she's here somewhere.' His thoughts raced. 'She's gone deeper into the Warens in search of a cure for Shargh wounds.' Miken's mouth fell open and Kest felt scarcely less surprised by his own certainty.

'I think you're right,' said Tresen slowly.

Miken rubbed his face. 'The further caverns are unmapped.'

'Yes, but I know Kira's been to some of them before,' said Kest, 'and I have too since the first attack. There are Writings there, very old and all but rotted. If there *is* a cure for Shargh wounds, it might be amongst them.'

'*If,*' echoed Miken. 'That's less concern to me now than the possibility of her becoming lost,' he said, and strode off.

Kest hurried after him. 'She once told me she had a good memory of the way,' he said.

'That was before her heart was torn out.'

Kest caught his arm. 'I'll go, Clanleader.'

Miken eyed him grimly. 'And what makes you think, *you* won't get lost, Commander Kest?'

'On my last visit there I took the precaution of drawing a map.'

Miken stared at him for a moment then his face cracked in a grin. 'That was *very* wise of you, Commander Kest.'

Kest picked up one of the lamps from the table and checked the oil. 'Don't wait up,' he said by way of farewell.

2

Kira sat back on her heels, arched her aching back, and wiped the mottled fragments of paper from her fingers. It was little wonder the Writings had decayed; even the walls were covered in a moisture-loving growth. It was not moss, for there was no light, and moss was not slimy and rank-smelling.

She wiped her hands on her trousers again and froze as one of her father's rebukes echoed in her ears. For a moment she was caught, a litter-mouse under a frostking's shadow, then she struggled to her feet and went back to the cavern entrance.

Which way? Ahead lay utter darkness, while behind the wounded died. She went on. Once she would have scorned a light and found her way by touch and memory, but she held the lamp before her now, too tired to trust herself. At least the floor was smooth and the journeying easy with only the occasional drip of water to break the silence, and irregular drafts of air to remind her of the world above.

But there were no forest scents or bird calls, and she felt their absence keenly. In fact, there was nothing in the surrounding stone to ease her heart or distract her from the plight of the dying. Even the slimy growths had disappeared. How much further could she go tonight? Or was it day? She shook her head. She must keep moving, not think of what had passed, or what might come.

She was a Healer and there were wounded to be healed, and she was Kasheron's line. He had sundered a people to heal, fought his way south to heal; healing was

14

all that mattered. The cavern openings dwindled and the ache in her bones grew. Surely Kasheron had not come this far? The caverns were too distant to be convenient for storage, or for anything else, for that matter, *except to hide something precious*.

She slumped against the wall to consider the possibility and unexpectedly felt grittiness. Kira stared at the stone in confusion. It was covered in soot. Her heart quickened. There was a hole in the stone where a bracket had been fixed, and a bracket meant people had come here often enough to warrant a permanent light. She blinked the sweat from her eyes, raised the lamp, and strained ahead. There was a shadow of another cavern there, right on the edge of the lamp-light, and she hurried forward.

It was a huge and she stopped in its entranceway. Wooden shelving had been hammered into the stone from floor to ceiling and stacked high with cloth-wrapped bundles. Kira's eyes widened. Kasheron's folk had established a worthy hiding place indeed. She set the lamp down, lifted a bundle from the shelves and carefully unwound the oiled cloth. Her hands shook as she stroked the paper, knowing that Kasheron's followers may have been the last people to touch the sheaf, perhaps even Kasheron himself!

The paper lacked the ridges of patchet paper and confirmed that this sheaf, at least, came from the north, but Kira's excitement soon cooled as she read page after page of the provisioning and placement of the longhouses; records of what the octads offered as gathering; and lists of storage space assigned each clan. It was recorded in Tremen, but strangely spelled and phrased, and at the top of each page, written in faded ink, was a date: *Season twenty, Allogrenia*.

Twenty seasons after Kasheron came south, she deduced. The Tremen no longer measured time from their arrival in the forest but the date held her gaze, and she wondered what else had changed in the north. Had Terak's legacy of barbarity endured as Kasheron's legacy of healing had? Did the Terak Kutan still kill like the Shargh killed?

She stared at the shelves and was overcome with a terrible sense of dread. No matter what herbal lore lay in this cavern or in other caverns, it could not prevail against a sword. Only a sword could defeat a sword and that meant killing had already won.

Kira snapped the sheaf shut, bundled the oiled cloth around it, and thrust it back on the shelf. Killing would *never* be mightier than that which gave life! The idea was seeded by weariness, nothing more. She jerked another sheaf from the shelf but it was full of lists too. And the next, and the next.

She soon gave up looking at every page and flicked the paper over quickly, scanning for herbal or healing words, and she was on her fifth sheaf when a page came adrift. She swore, thinking her carelessness had torn it loose, but it was covered in lines not writing.

The lamplight flickered, and she leaned forward. It was a map of the Warens, she realized, but she was too exhausted to feel excited. It showed the stores and the training rooms, the Water Cavern, and the tunnel she had used to reach this cavern: the *Sarnia Room*.

It was the same name as the caves where Sanaken and Feseren had died, and her stomach knotted. Why use the same name as the Terak Kutan's stone city of death? The map showed that the tunnel went on and that more caverns opened off it. There were other Warens entrances too, apart

16

from Nogren, if that was what the open-ended lines meant. She counted quickly: one entrance to the north, and two to the north-west.

The light dimmed, and she glanced up at the lamp. Stinking heart-rot! The wick leaned drunkenly as it sucked up the last of oil and even as she stared in horror, the flame flickered and went out. Kira remained frozen in the darkness. She could not even see her hand in front of her face. Where had the cavern's entrance been? Which way had she faced? For a moment, her mind was as dark as the cavern, and then she managed to visualize the cavern's layout.

She rose carefully, stretched her arms out sideways and held her breath as she took two large strides to her right. Nothing. Her heart pounded, and she took a third. Still nothing. Maybe she was wrong, maybe . . . Her knuckles skimmed the rough cloth of a sheaf and she all but swooned. Thank the 'green!

She turned slowly and moved forward, sliding each foot gingerly along the floor. Her hand trailed into space again and her teeth chattered in panic, but after two more steps, her fingers found the cool stone of the entranceway, and she edged around it, careful to keep it at her right shoulder. The way back lay before her and the relief was so great she half slid down the wall.

For a while she crouched on the stone, panting as if she had sprinted between the Eights, then she eased herself down and stretched out on her back. The silence was absolute, and she wondered if this was what the dead endured. No light, no sound, no warmth, no birdsong, no rustle of leaves in summer winds, no scuttle of gold and green across the forest floor. Nothing.

She wanted to weep for Kandor and for all the others she had lost, and she wanted to weep for herself, but she had forgotten how. She was lost too, as empty as the stone around her. She curled into a ball, closed her eyes, and slept.

Kest came to a stop and glanced from the dwindling bulb of nut oil to the vast darkness ahead. If he did not turn back soon, he would be making the return journey like a blind man, *if* there were a return journey. He had come to the end of his rough map eleven caverns ago and had counted the openings to his left since to keep his bearings.

He had never come this far before and was surprised by how dry the air was. Dry air but no Kira, and doubt gnawed. Perhaps she had slipped through some crevice he had missed or looped back and was now safely ensconced in the training rooms. He grunted and started forward again. He was a fool if he believed so. Kira would turn back only if she found the cure for the stinking rot of Shargh wounds, and the chances of that were remote.

Sweat dripped from his face as he strode over the stone and his arm ached from holding the lamp aloft. Curse the darkness and her stubbornness! Miken must be mad to consider making her leader! She was like a child who had no regard for anyone or anything except herself. He swore again, but his fear was greater than his anger, burrowing into him ever deeper like a wood-grub.

What if she *were* lost? He remembered how she had woken in his bed, the sense of her as she had caressed the chimes, the way she had laughed up at him over the silverjack. If she were lost, there was no one else. Only a bare half dozen of Kashclan had healing skills that set them apart, but there was no one like her; no other Feailner.

The lamp picked up a tumble of stone ahead. It was the first rockfall he had seen in the otherwise smooth tunnel and then his heart raced as the stone resolved into a prone figure. Stinking heart-rot! He hastened forward and dropped to his knees beside her, expecting the coldness of death, but she was warm, and his relief flashed to anger.

He shook her savagely. 'Get up!' he ordered. She scrabbled away from him in terror and Kest felt a stab of remorse. 'I'm sorry I startled you,' he muttered.

Kira pushed her hair from her face and left a dusty smudge on her forehead. 'I ran out of oil,' she said, as if her being alone deep in the Warens' darkness were inconsequential.

He caught her arm and hauled her up. 'Come. You're needed.'

'We have to search the cavern,' she said, gesturing to the gaping opening behind her.

'You've been away a long time, Kira,' he said, struggling to keep his voice calm. 'The wounded need you. Come.'

'No!'

Kest wrenched her forward, so that her face all but touched his. 'It isn't what *you* want anymore, Kira,' he ground out. 'Don't you understand? It's what the *Tremen* want. You're no longer free to go traipsing off when the mood takes you; you're all we've got left. You're Kasheron's blood and Kasheron's legacy. That gives you *obligations*, Kira! It gives you *responsibilities*, something I know you aren't familiar with. Now we're going back, whether you're willing or not!'

His grip on her arm was punishing and he loomed over her, like her father had in the Herbery, *before the blow*. She threw herself backwards in panic, breaking his grip, and as her feet went from under her, her boot caught him in the groin. She landed on her backside with a painful thump and, as Kest doubled over, the tunnel filled with harsh wheezing as he struggled to breathe.

'That . . . was a . . . neat trick,' he managed to say. 'Who . . . taught you that?'

'I . . . no one. I'm sorry I hurt you.'

'That is a . . . great comfort.' He managed to straighten, and she took a step backwards. There was fear in her face, but also a fierce determination, and he regretted being the cause of both.

'If I go back now, Kest, it will make no difference to the injured. They will die anyway. I know it, you know it, and probably most of the Tremen know it by now too. But this cave,' she jerked her head toward it, 'is filled with Writings. I think it was Kasheron's main store. If the cure for Shargh wounds isn't there, then I don't think it's anywhere.'

'We're going to . . . run out of oil,' said Kest, still having trouble breathing. 'We will find nothing in the dark, including . . . our way back.'

'There are holes in the wall where lamps have been fixed. People must have come here and stayed and that means there will be a store of oil nearby.' She paused, and the lamp's dimming light picked up the flash of her eyes. 'I need your help, Kest. I need your help to save the wounded. Will you give it to me?'

For a long moment Kest simply stared at her, and then he nodded. 'Maybe Miken isn't mad after all,' he muttered.

3

Tresen hauled himself up from the floor next to Farek's mattress, rubbed his numb backside and forced his cramped legs to straighten. His Protector comrade had slid into a fretful sleep some time ago, but Tresen had been too weary to move, unlike his father. Miken had gone back to his longhouse.

Tresen hobbled off towards Kira's alcove where he knew there was a jug of water and bathing bowl. The pins and needles in his foot dissipated as he limped along, but not his dread. Kira should have been back by now. Where in the 'green was she?

The jug was full, for Kira hadn't had time to do anything but tend the wounded, and he stared at it dully then grimaced at the sight of his grimy cuffs. What he would give for a proper wash, clean clothing, and the chance to sleep in a bed not intent on stabbing him to death. Why the Protectors persevered with sere grass mattresses was beyond him. Maybe it was some sort of test of endurance no one had thought to tell him about.

He had no right to complain though. Arlen had offered to take his place for a time, so he could have gone back to his longhouse with Miken. And it wasn't as if Arlen weren't a careful and competent Healer; he was Kashclan after all, but Tresen had chosen to stay to keep an eye on Kira. Well, a fine job he had done of that!

He stared at her mattress with its small pile of clothing at one end, and then at the wooden bench with its bowl and water jug. There was not even a chair in the room and the alcove's emptiness seemed to amplify what Kira had suffered. What if he had lost everyone? What if he had seen Miken and Tenerini dead, and Mikini murdered before his eyes?

Hot tears spilled down his cheeks. How did Kira draw breath, put one foot in front of the other, go on? He emptied the jug of water over his head and gasped as icy trickles found his collar and zigzagged down his back. Well, that had certainly woken him up!

'Protector Tresen?'

He started, then went to the hanging and pushed it aside. It was Kesilini, her clothes clean and her neatly braided hair gleaming in the lamplight, and Tresen mopped ineffectually at his face with his sleeve. 'You are looking better,' he said, then regretted his allusion to Merek's death. 'Do you seek Kest?' he added hurriedly.

'No . . . yes. I sought you, but if you know where my brother is, I would be pleased if you'd tell me.'

'I *think* he's with Kira, but I don't know where *she* is,' admitted Tresen.

Kesilini nodded, her face carefully composed. 'Actually, I came to help you, or at least to offer my help. I helped prepare some of the herbs earlier and I've helped with women in childbirth. I know it isn't the same, but I could prepare bandages or clean wounds, *if* you show me how, or watch while you get some sleep.'

She had the same blue eyes as Kest, he noticed, but so much sadder. 'Thank you, Kesilini. I would be glad of your help.' He led her back to the most severely wounded. 'The men here have been given everest and will sleep at least another day, but you can help me give the others honeyed-water.' He went to the table, ladled a dollop of honey into a water jug and stirred.

22

Kesilini followed, her confusion clear. 'Only honeyed-water? I would have thought . . .' She colored. 'I'm sorry, I didn't mean to question . . . I'm not a Healer.'

Tresen tapped the spoon on the side of the jug and watched the last of the honey slide off. 'You thought we would be doing more for them?' he asked softly. 'You're right, Kesilini,' he added, failing to keep the bitterness from his voice. 'We've cleansed the wounds with sorren, and stitched them, and bound them with falzon. Ordinarily that would be enough, but these aren't ordinary wounds. They're Shargh wounds, and Shargh wounds rot despite our healing. All we can do is stave off thirst.'

Kesilini's eyes widened. 'Are you saying there's no cure for Shargh wounds?' Tresen hesitated, knowing he had already said too much, and Kesilini leaned closer, her voice falling to a hiss. 'Are you saying that Healer Kiraon can't heal them?'

'I won't lie to you, Kesilini,' he said softly, 'not after all you've lost, but what I say *mustn't* go beyond this room.' She nodded jerkily. 'The Shargh use something on their blades that causes wounds to rot. Even small wounds rot. Kasheron's people knew of a cure, but the knowing has been lost. Unless we find it again, we can't heal the wounded.'

Kesilini's face had blanched as pale as her hair. 'Then they will die,' she murmured brokenly.

'There *is* hope. Everest seems to slow the fester, and I think Kira's gone deep into the Warens to search for the oldest Writings. Kest's gone after her.'

Kesilini caught his arm. 'There's danger?'

'Not from the Shargh, but the Warens are a tangle of tunnels and caverns, and completely dark. They've never been completely mapped either and I know Kira's exhausted. She's barely slept since the attack.'

'Then why did you let her go? If she gets lost, if they *both* get lost, or injured, or . . .'

'Do you think she asked my permission?'

'You should have—' started Kesilini.

'Seen her go and stopped her? Yes, I *should* have. And Maxen *should* have taken Sarkash's advice and postponed the Feast of Turning. And the Protectors *should* have patrolled the First Eight.' He slammed the spoon down on the table. 'All these things *should* have happened, Kesilini, but they didn't, and they can't be undone. Kira's choice was to stay here and watch the wounded die or go into the darkness. Kest's choice was the same. Which do you think they *should* have chosen?'

Kesilini dropped her head and a tear slid off her cheek onto her tunic to leave a damp line.

Tresen pushed his hand through his hair. 'I'm sorry, Kesilini. It's probably best you *do* go back to your longhouse.'

'No,' she mumbled. 'I will stay. I . . . I thank you for telling me these things. They were right to go.' She gave a tremulous smile. 'Leader Maxen planned to make Merek leader after him, but I never thought it was right. It should always have been Kiraon. I've seen her heal. She fights to heal in the same way that Kest fights.' Tears started afresh and she wiped them away. 'It's just that I'm frightened I will lose Kest too.'

Tresen touched her briefly on the hand. 'We are *all* frightened of losing those we love, Kesilini.'

A flock of springleslips darted away through the canopy, their blue and yellow plumage bright in the new sun's dapples, but mist still streamered through the trees, and Miken chaffed his hands as he stood at his longhouse's doorway. All but one of the clanleaders were seated in the hall behind him, busy with their breakfast of nutbread and dried mundleberries that Tenerini had set ready, and the fresh lemonleaf tea Mikini had brewed.

Tenerini was at the edge of the trees, filling the cups of the clanleaders' Protector escorts and sending Mikini and Mira back and forth to the longhouse on all manner of errands. Miken watched the springleslips but his ears were tuned to the conversations behind him: *the routes of the Protector patrols; how gathering was to be accomplished; the likelihood of further attacks.* The clanleaders were anxious about leaving their longhouses even for a short time.

He glanced back into the hall and caught Marren's eye, and the Morclan leader's brows rose in an easily guessed at question: would the clanleaders support Kira as leader? It was a question Miken had pondered most of the night. Meetings to appoint new leaders were inevitably difficult. It meant the previous leader had died and one of the clans present was in mourning.

It was doubly difficult this time because Maxen enjoyed the loyalty of most of the clanleaders, and his death had been both shocking and untimely. It had been different with Maxen's predecessor. Kashmin had been old and ailing, and the council had had time to consider his replacement.

Miken rocked on the balls of his feet in an effort to contain his impatience. At least Dakresh was consistent; he was *always* the last to arrive. Miken stepped out into

25

the crisp air and took several quick paces up and down on the dewy grass. Perhaps it had been a mistake to call a council at all. Perhaps he should have waited for someone else to do it.

Many of the clanleaders saw him as Maxen's adversary and might withhold their support for Kira because she was clan-kin. There were other sensitivities too. Apart from he and Marren, the clanleaders had agreed with Maxen that no threat existed to Allogrenia, and that meant they would have to justify their decisions or admit they were wrong.

His lips settled into a grim line. Clanleader Farish would not because he had been slaughtered at the Bough. Miken wondered who Tarclan blamed for their clanleader's death. Certainly not Farish; it was always easier to turn away from the pain of a self-inflicted wound than admit fault. Tarclan's new leader, Kemrick, was already inside but Miken knew little of him, apart from him being a lot older than Farish. Whatever he was like, Miken hoped he could think for himself, not mouth Berendash's views as Farish had.

There was movement in the trees as a new patrol arrived and Dakresh hobbled stiffly towards him over the grass. 'Kashclan welcomes Sherclan,' said Miken formally.

'Sherclan thanks Kashclan,' said Dakresh, as he peered up at him from under silvered brows. Miken escorted him inside to his seat, took his own and gulped down his tea. He scalded his mouth but his thoughts were already on his fellow councilors.

He *had* been right to call the council, he decided, despite the risks to Kira's claim on the leadership, *and* the need for the clans to grieve their losses. The Shargh threat remained and that meant new leaders must be appointed, both in the Bough and in the Warens, and a strategy for protection agreed on and put in place.

He rose and cleared his throat, and the conversations died away. 'Kashclan welcomes Clanleaders Dakresh, Kemrick, Tenedren, Ketten, Berendash, Sanden and Marren to council,' he began formally, careful to put Marren last to avoid highlighting their usual accord. He waited for the gathering to finish its traditional response and then bowed to Kemrick. 'The Clancouncil mourns the loss of Clanleader Farish. May he rest easy beneath the 'green.'

Kemrick rose. 'Tarclan has given him to Wesgren. He is the sun and air; he is the roots and soil.'

'May the alwaysgreen Shelter him,' responded the council.

Kemrick resumed his seat and Marren rose. 'The Clancouncil mourns the loss of Tremen Leader Maxen. May he rest easy beneath the 'green.'

'Kashclan has given him to Sogren,' responded Miken. 'He is the sun and air; he is the roots and soil.'

'May the alwaysgreen Shelter him,' returned the council.

Miken stood again and solemnly surveyed the gathering. 'We have much to decide today, councilors. Let us begin.'

Kest swore under his breath as he flicked through a sheaf. His neck was stiff and he was as dry as husk, and there was still at least two-thirds of the cavern's contents to check. It must be midday outside, or so the growl of his stomach told him.

'How many lists of gatherings do you need?' he muttered. '*Season eleven, Season twelve, Season eighteen,*

Season twenty-three.' He squinted through the gloom at Kira crouched motionless over a sheaf. 'Found anything?'

She did not respond and he dragged himself upright, the pain in his groin reminding him of their earlier encounter. 'Kira?' Did she sleep? No. He crouched beside her and peered at the Writing. 'What is it?'

'Deaths,' she said softly. 'Babes and their mothers. So many . . .'

'*Season five,*' noted Kest. 'The early days of Allogrenia. They would have hunted out the silverjacks by then and probably been trying to live on pitchie seeds. Not the best diet for a carrying woman.' He looked at the pile of discarded sheafs to her side. 'Nothing on healing?'

Kira shook her head. 'Not yet.' She peered up at him. 'We have to keep searching, Kest. We won't have time to come back.'

'I know.' Did she think he was going to argue? They both knew that in a couple of days the wounded would be beyond their help and that they would relive Feseren's death over and over again.

'Have you got food?' he asked irritably.

She shook her head. 'I didn't think to bring any. I didn't think I would be away this long.'

'The problem with you is that you *don't* think.'

Her eyes flashed to his. 'And I suppose you do? Well, *Commander* Kest, I'm waiting for you to offer me that nice slice of nutbread you have in your pack.'

Kest quelled a retort and grabbed another armful of sheafs from the shelf. Dust motes danced in the lamplight and he sneezed. At least the store had held a large cask of oil, as Kira had predicted, and they would not have to fumble all the way back.

He threw the pile on the floor and made a start. 'You realize the council's meeting today to make you leader,' he said, as he flicked over the first page.

'I won't accept the leadership,' she said, without looking up.

'You don't have any choice.'

'I'm not worthy of it. They'll have to find someone else.' She gathered up the sheafs, wrapped them, and pushed them back on the shelf.

Kest sat back on his haunches. 'There *is* no one else.' She faced the shelves, but he saw her hands clench.

'I'm not worthy,' she repeated.

Kest wondered if he had been a fool to broach the subject of leadership; to remind her of why a new leader was needed. If the grief she had managed to contain spilled out it might rob her of her wits. Allogrenia must have a strong leader! Someone who took no action, or worse still, vacillated, would be worse than useless, no matter their healing skill.

'I killed Kandor.'

For a moment he thought he had misheard, then he scrambled to his feet and wrenched her around, holding her by the shoulders so she must face him. 'The Shargh killed those of the Bough!'

'*I* killed him!'

It was almost a shriek. Perhaps Kandor's death and the battle to heal the injured *had* unhinged her. 'Kira—'

She jerked from his grip, her eyes as bright as flames in the lamplight. 'He wanted to come with me, but I made him stay in the Bough. Don't you understand? I *made* him stay!'

Kest knew from Miken that Kira had been running *towards* the Bough when they had intercepted her. 'Why did you leave—' he began, then his mind raced as he recalled Maxen's fury at Merek's bonding, and Maxen's cold gaze as Kest had danced with Kira. Kest's eyes went to the bruise on her face, now faded to yellow-green, and the cut under her cheekbone, and his blood ran cold.

'By the 'green which Shelters us!' he muttered and took a steadying breath. 'I know what happened that night,' he said softly, 'and I know how you got this.' He touched her cheek with the back of his fingers. 'And I say this to you, Kiraon of Kashclan, that none of it was your fault. It wasn't your fault that your father had no love for you, or that he put his own ambition before the good of the Tremen. And it wasn't your fault that he broke every tenet of Tremen law against violence.'

Kira caught his hand. 'Pledge that you won't speak of this, Kest. Pledge!'

'I seem to spend a lot of time pledging to remain silent on things that everyone should know.'

She took a shuddering breath. 'My father was appointed leader by the Clancouncil and accepted by the Tremen people. Speaking of this will only bring shame upon us all. We need to work together now, not squabble amongst ourselves. We need to remember what it is that makes us Tremen, and to fight for its survival.'

'Spoken like a true leader.'

She flushed but held his eyes. 'Will you pledge?'

'I will pledge on condition you accept the Clancouncil's decision, whatever it might be.'

Her remarkable eyes shifted to emerald green and then back to gold, then she nodded and Kest brought her hand to his lips. 'I shall enjoy working with you, Tremen Leader Kiraon.'

4

A single column of smoke rose over the grasslands, visible the length and breadth of the Grounds. No wind blew and no wing-beat frayed or softened it, so that it reached high into the sky before it skewed sideways to spread its stain.

The pyre had been set on the edge of the Grounds, where the land rose and broke into the stony steps of the Cashgars. There, a single cave-mouth gaped to mark the place of the Last Telling. It was where the Sky Chiefs' breath came closest to the earth, and where their thoughts had once seeded the minds of Tellers. It was also where the spirit quit its shell of flesh most easily, to make its journey skyward.

The crowd's wails had been silenced by the ritual lighting of the pyre and now they swayed as the flames took hold. The gather-wood was brittle from countless days under the sun, and the flames soon licked at the wolf-skins that enclosed Erboran's corpse, so that his burning flesh soured the smoke.

The acrid plumes engulfed Arkendrin, who had positioned himself too close to the pyre, but he stood his ground, eyes smarting, mouth clamped shut to silence a cough. His brother's profile was dark against the orange of the flames, and as the wood broke and settled, Erboran's jaw sagged open in a macabre grin.

Arkendrin's teeth clenched. Even in death his brother mocked him! Arkendrin's gaze swung to Palansa at the pyre's head. She shimmered like a spirit-shadow in the heat-warped air; chin held high while her stinking belly

31

ripened like ground-fruit. She stood in the chief's place, in *his* place. How could a thing unborn be chief? He sucked in a lungful of smoke and was racked by a hacking cough.

Two sword strokes lay between him and the chiefship and his muscles ached to take what was rightfully his. Erboran's skin blistered and cracked, but Arkendrin barely noticed as his thoughts buzzed like blackflies. If he claimed he had bedded Palansa *before* she had joined with his brother, then the seed that grew in her belly would be his, *and* the chiefship.

But he would not be believed; his cursed mother had seen to that! She had made it known amongst the sorchas high and low on the spur, that Palansa had bled in Erboran's bed at their joining.

Tarkenda had always sided with Erboran against him, and now she used Palansa to take the chiefship for herself! His fingers twitched, and his muscles bunched, as if about to spring. Half the Shargh already favored him as chief and it would take little to bring the rest behind him: just the death of the healer-creature, or the miscarry of his brother's seed. Killing the creature of the Telling would be simpler, and then he would take Palansa whether she willed it or not. Death of the young during birthing was unfortunate but not uncommon.

He felt his mother's gaze upon him and forced his face to solemnity. The air was unbearably close, the stale end of another hot day, and he craved the touch of rain against his skin. His muscles bunched again, and with the slightest dip of his head and touch to his forehead, he strode away across the Grounds. He had danced attendance on the great dead chief long enough!

As soon as he was clear, he broke into a run, ignoring

the slide of sweat over his body as he forced his feet into rhythm with his pounding heart. The cracked margins of the Thanawah stretched ahead, and he turned and ran parallel with its sluggish flow until he came to the stands of slitweed.

The blood roared in his ears and he stopped and waited until the sounds of the Grounds intruded: the ebis' hungry bellows behind him; the slitweeds' sere mutter; a water-toad's growling croak. A shrunken moon bobbed on the water, its outline blurring on the Thanawah's oily surface. Arkendrin glared at it. So it was with the Sky Chiefs! Their intentions seeming one thing one moment but being something else entirely. They had birthed him into the chief's family, *a season behind the first-born*, then taken the first-born home to the cloudlands, *and left his seed behind*.

But no more! Before the moon was full again, Arkendrin would be back under the cursed trees in the south-west forests, and this time he would capture the healer-creature. Not that it was his fault the creature still lived. Erboran had led badly and even in death had thwarted him, forcing him to abandon the attack to bring the *great chief's* body home.

Well, the sending ceremony was over, and he would not be idling away the three mourning moons while Palansa's claim on the chiefship grew as big as her belly. The sooner the thing of the Telling was dead, the sooner he could prize the chiefship from Palansa and his mother's fists.

His chest heaved again and his hand flashed to his dagger as something moved. It was the water-toad, its eyes as yellow as those of the foul thing of the Telling. It hopped closer, muscles rippling under its glistening skin, and Arkendrin slammed his heel down.

The toad's skin popped, and he ground the quivering mass to a jelly, then booted its remains into the water, and strode off. The moon's reflection shattered and as its shards drew together again, the toad's blood drifted across its face like smoke from the funeral pyre.

The night was quiet but Irdodun was far from at ease as he salted the peeling skins of the grahen carcasses on the makeshift spit. His gaze was more often on Arkendrin's back than on the meal he prepared. The fire-light glanced off the eyes of the wolf Arkendrin had slain, making them glow in imitation of life, even as its body stiffened.

The pelt was lush and Irdodun wondered whether Arkendrin would claim it for himself. He had made no move to skin the beast, just stood and stared out over the Grounds. Irdodun poked at the coals to even the heat and imagined the pelt strewn across his sorcha floor or thickening his bed covers. Urpalin coughed, jerking Irdodun from his reverie, and he scowled down at the fire.

'Will I skin the beast for you, Chief?' asked Urpalin, his eyes also on the wolf. Irdodun kept his gaze on the fire, not trusting himself to look at Urpalin's scrawny face and he sensed Orthaken tense too.

Arkendrin was barely aware of his companions. His body still throbbed from the chase and the wolf's blood was still wet on his shirt. The cave of the Last Teller lay at his back, and the sky was pierced with a moon as sharp as ebis horn that gave little light, but he needed *no* light to know the place of each sorcha on the slope, each pool and eddy n the Thanawah, Grenwah, and Shunawah, each rock and roothold of burrel, targasso, and stone-tree.

The Grounds were dotted with cooking fires, but he stared beyond them to the south-west, to where the gold-eyed creature lived, and breathed, and prospered. 'I won't wait three moons,' he said, swinging back to the fire. 'I won't let my people suffer just to honor a man who takes his ease with the Sky Chiefs.'

'The Chief-mother will say Erboran must have his three moons of mourning,' said Irdodun. 'She will use it against you.'

Arkendrin paced to and fro on the edge of the fire. 'The curse of the last Telling grows stronger by the day. We cannot afford three moons of lounging in our sorchas for a corpse. The creature must be destroyed before it destroys us.'

'You speak as a chief should,' said Urpalin.

'We need to know where the creature hides,' said Irdodun. 'It wasn't in the place we burned. We must know where it is.'

'We could send watchers,' suggested Urpalin.

Arkendrin's teeth flashed. 'When Urgundin was taken, the Sky Chiefs granted me a boon. I've heard tell it is so with those they favor.'

Irdodun leaned forward. 'A boon?'

'When first we found the creature, the treemen shouted the creature's name. We don't need to find the creature, only a treeman who knows of it.'

'It will be simple to make him speak,' said Urpalin, and patted his dagger. 'But we don't know their tongue. How are we to understand what the treeman says?'

Arkendrin's gaze swung to Orthaken and he started. 'Orthaken, your blood-tie, Irason, told me what the name meant, for once he traded with our Ashmiri brothers. The Ashmiri trade far, and even know words of the filthy northerners. Irason knows them too. Bring him to the edge of the forests and wait for me there.'

Orthaken licked his lips. 'Chief Arkendrin, Irason is old. There is much he no longer remembers. What if it isn't enough?'

'It will be enough.'

Palansa wrung the water from the last of her clothes, dumped the wet bundles in her basket, and struggled upright. There were many women at the Grenwah's washpools, their chatter ebbing and flowing on the sunny air, and she nodded to them as she propped the basket on her hip and turned up the bank.

She was glad to be done with her chores. Her belly made crouching awkward and she was relieved to be away from the curious eyes of the other women.

She stopped at the top of the bank to swing the basket onto her other hip and Ormadon appeared at her side. She glanced at the old warrior in irritation. Didn't Tarkenda even trust the women at their washing?

'I will carry the basket for you, Chief-wife,' he said.

'There is no need.' They walked for a while in silence, Palansa's gaze on the sky. It was cloudless again and the grasses crisp underfoot. If only the Sky Chiefs sent rain.

'And what do the washer-women say?' asked Ormadon.

'Only the usual gossip. I'm sure it's of no interest to you, *unless* you've come to like women's work.'

'Gossip is always of interest, Chief-wife. Women speak loudly of what their join-husbands' whisper. The one furthest upstream; whose blood-tie is she?'

Palansa glanced back. 'Ermashin's. She's joined to his uncle's second son.'

'Of what did she speak?'

'She complained that her join-husband gives her no pleasure in bed. She says he should just be called a husband because he is no longer capable of joining with her.' Palansa glanced sideways at him, but Ormadon's ruddy face remained impassive. 'She says she might try a younger man tonight, as her join-husband's away,' added Palansa mischievously.

Ormadon's eyes narrowed. 'Did she say where her join-husband was?'

'No, but I've noticed Arkendrin's sorcha has been empty these last few days,' said Palansa, sobering. 'I know he goes beyond the Grenwah hunting, but it's his habit to be back by nightfall.'

'Perhaps he returns while you sleep.'

'The fire circle is cold.'

'It is good you are observant, Chief-wife. It bodes well for the health of your son, the next chief.'

Palansa shifted her washing basket back to her other hip as they started up the spur and gazed at the sweep of desiccated pasture lands around her. 'What does it mean, Ormadon?'

'Erlken tells me Orthaken has taken Irason to the south-west forests.'

They neared the first of the sorchas and Palansa lowered her voice. 'Irason can scarcely walk, so crippled is he with old-man's ache. His join-wife spends half her time grubbing for oil-root in the targasso, but it doesn't seem to do him any good.'

'I don't think they've taken him south-west for his swiftness,' murmured Ormadon. His gaze moved between Orthaken and Urpalin's deserted sorchas and his hand fastened on his flatsword as marwings flapped overhead.

Palansa tightened her grip on her basket took but said nothing, just concentrated on the steep path that wound up the spur.

'Before his strength was taken, Irason travelled far,' said Ormadon softly. 'He learned the tongues of other people.'

The babe pummeled at Palansa's lungs and she stopped to catch her breath. She was tempted to accept Ormadon's offer to carry the basket after all, but decided it was better his hands were free. She set the basket down and waited for the babe to quiet.

There was only one reason Arkendrin would trouble himself with a Voiceless, crippled old man, low on the spur. 'He seeks the gold-eyed Healer of the Last Telling,' she muttered. 'He thinks killing her will deliver him the chiefship.'

'Killing her or killing the next chief,' said Ormadon. 'He thinks it will be simpler to kill her, but if that fails . . .'

'I'm not afraid of him,' said Palansa fiercely.

'There are many who aren't afraid of the red scum infesting the Thanawah's drinking holes, but it still injures them,' said Ormadon.

There was a short silence and Palansa's hands clenched protectively over her belly. 'What should I do?'

'Let the Chief-mother guide you and I'll send Erlken to keep you company for a while. I think it's time I listened to what the sorchas' tell.'

5

Miken felt as if he had been confined in the Kashclan's hall for days, not since dawn, and with no release in sight. Half the councilors were passionate that Kira become leader, and the other half equally passionate that she not. Arguments surged to and fro like the Drinkwater in flood but with no sign of abatement.

He refilled his cup and glanced out the window. The light told him it was well past midday and that the still morning had given way to a breezy afternoon. Castellas and severs swayed but their rustlings were drowned out by the hubbub in the room.

Dakresh was on his feet now, waving his finger under Marren's nose, and Miken decided it was time to call a halt. The debate had reached the stage where everything had been said anyway and was being repeated with different words. Miken set his cup down with a loud chink and rose. 'Councilors! Councilors!' The noise faltered and faces turned to him. 'I think it's time we made a decision.'

'It was time we made a decision mid-morning,' growled Dakresh.

'We need to make a *good* decision,' retorted Marren, glaring at him, 'not *any* decision, and good decision-making takes time.'

'So does bad,' muttered someone.

'I could have called for the dividing some time ago,' acknowledged Miken, 'and I would have if we'd debated foraging rights or the exchange of goods between longhouses. But I need hardly remind you that we are deciding something far more important, and that whoever we appoint Tremen Leader today, must have the support of *all* of us, not just half,' he said, and stared at each councilor in turn.

'It's clear you don't have the numbers, clanleader,' said Dakresh. 'Let's just get on with it, so we can move to the Warens leadership and be getting back to our own longhouses.'

Marren's chair grated back as he stood. 'It isn't just a matter of numbers, Clanleader Dakresh, but of who is best suited to lead the Bough.'

'Precisely,' snapped Dakresh. 'And a girl of barely seventeen seasons isn't *best suited*, even if she *is* a good Healer. The next leader should have been Merek. He was the only one of Maxen's seed with the strength of will to see us through this and it's one of the great tragedies of this whole sorry business that he was taken too.'

Miken opened his mouth to protest but shut it again, knowing that nothing he said now would improve the situation. Another figure rose: Kemrick of Tarclan who, until this moment, had been silent. Miken had known nothing of Farish's replacement before his appointment and he knew little now, beyond Kemrick being an intensely private man given to solitary wandering. He was a strange choice by Tarclan, especially after Farish's brashness.

'Clancouncilors,' began Kemrick, 'forgive me if I am naive, for I have spent little time in these debates, whereas you are all obviously well-practiced. It seems to me that the issues being debated here today are really quite simple. As a Tremen, my understanding is that the Bough is the centre of all healing. Is that not so?'

His gaze shifted slowly around the councilors and there were nods of agreement. 'And it is also my understanding that Kiraon of Kashclan is the best surviving Healer in

Allogrenia.' Again came the murmurs of assent. 'Then it follows, does it not, that she should be Leader of the Bough.'

'It isn't as simple as that, Clanleader Kemrick,' said Berendash. 'It isn't Kiraon's healing skill which is in question here, but her strength and strategic ability.'

'Strength and strategic ability?' murmured Kemrick. 'I rather thought they were the preserve of the Warens.' He smiled gently to ease the bluntness of his words. 'I am, as I have said, unpracticed in the ways of debates, but I am well-versed in the histories of Allogrenia. How and why we came to be here have always been of interest to me, and I have spent considerable time studying the sheafs stowed in the Warens.

'What they tell me is that Kasheron gave his heart to healing, but his head understood the wisdom of keeping the sword. We have been fortunate to have had so many seasons of peace to enjoy his legacy of healing, but now we must call upon the other half of what he bequeathed us.

'It seems to me that the decision that faces us is not who will be Leader of the Bough, for we agree that Kiraon of Kashclan is the best Healer, but who will be command the Protectors in the Warens.'

There was absolute silence and Kemrick nodded to each councilor in turn. 'I thank you for hearing me,' he said, and sat down.

Miken schooled his face to blandness. 'I thank you, Clanleader Kemrick. Are there any further contributions? No? Then I suggest we divide.'

'I see no reason to waste time in two divisions when one will suffice,' snapped Berendash, and glanced around the table. 'I take it we are in agreement in appointing Kashclanswoman Kiraon to the leadership of the Bough?'

41

There was a mutter of assent. 'Then let us focus on who is to command the Warens. The Protectors of my longhouse tell me their preferred commander is Kest of Morclan.'

'As do mine,' added Tenedren.

'And mine,' said Sanden.

'What say the other clans?' asked Miken.

'Kest obviously has the confidence of Morclan,' said Marren. His eyes slid to Dakresh.

'I have no objection,' grunted Dakresh. 'He is young in his seasons, but old in his thinking. The men like him and that's important if they must spill their blood for him.'

'For us,' corrected Kemrick gently.

Miken watched the last of the clanleaders' Protector escorts disappear amongst the trees. He still could not quite believe what had happened. 'So Kira's to be leader,' said Tenerini, coming to his side.

Miken slipped his arm around her. 'And Kest is to replace Sarkash.'

'He's a good choice.'

'But not Kira?'

Tenerini was intent on the springleslips hunting bark beetles amongst the castellas, but the kink in her brows told him she was troubled. 'Kira,' she said, and sighed. 'Kira needs time to grieve and to heal herself, but if she's Leader of the Bough, she will have no time, not even if *when* this is over.'

'*When* this is over, there will be less need of healing,' said Miken. 'She will be able to visit Sogren and Wessogren to say her farewells, to come to accept what happened, to live in peace. She might even bond and find happiness that way.'

42

'It might be too late. Kandor was everything to her.' Tenerini looked up at him. 'We should have fought harder to have her here with us, Miken, *and* Kandor.'

Miken ran his finger down her cheek. 'Yes, how well we see when we look over our shoulders.' His mouth settled into a hard line. 'But we both know Maxen would never have relented. The more we asked, the more he delighted in refusing.'

'Yet he had no love for either of them.'

Miken's arm tightened round her and he kissed her forehead. 'No, but he enjoyed having power over them, particularly Kira. And while he had Kandor, he had all the power in the world.'

Tenerini snorted. 'Well, he has none now, and I'm glad. The only good that's come from this horror, may the 'green forgive me, is that Kira is free of him at last.'

Miken looked at her in surprise. 'That's an unworthy sentiment, Tenerini.'

'Yes, I know, but an honest one. And you're the only person I dare voice it to.'

'Ah, then it's fortunate we are bonded and bound to keep each other's secrets.' Miken stared out into the fading light as birds winged overhead in search of roosts. Springleslips' shrill cries mixed with those of tippets and honeysprites, but away to the east he heard another bird-cry, eerie and other-worldly. The mira kiraon's. He knew it was distorted by distance, but he shivered. 'I need go back to the Warens,' he said abruptly.

Tenerini stiffened. 'Not this night surely? You were only there yesterday.'

'I know, but Kira had gone off into the tunnels and I didn't see her. I need to speak with her about the leadership.' *And to reassure himself she was well.*

'Can't it wait? Go tomorrow instead, Miken, with an escort.'

'There isn't much risk while the moon is small,' he said, and he would rather leave the Protectors here with his family and clan-kin.

'You think the next attack will come with the next full moon?'

Miken hesitated, but Tenerini was not a child to be fed only honey. 'Both attacks have been at the full moon,' he said slowly. 'And it makes sense for a people who unfamiliar with the forest. Even Tremen have been known to get lost on cloudful nights.'

'The next full moon,' whispered Tenerini, as her gaze on the darkening trees.

Miken drew her back into the hall and shut the door. The longhouse was full of light and the comforting smells of espin smoke and nutbread, and the voices of Kashclan as they prepared their evening meals.

He watched Tenerini join them at the cookingplace and slipped on his pack. The Shargh had gone straight to the Bough last time, to the leader and his family, but there was nothing to say they would not attack the longhouses. He stepped out into the dusk and set off at speed.

Kest's voice came from a long way off. 'I think I've found something.' Kira jerked upright. She had no recollection of the last few moments and wondered if she had slept. She pushed her hair from her eyes and grimaced at the smell of her musty hands. 'It's a list of herbs from Kenclan octad. Something about fireweed and—' Kira sprang to her feet and all but fell on top of him as she snatched the sheaf from his hands. 'There's no need—' he objected.

'I'm sorry, I'm sorry,' she muttered, as she read feverishly. Her head swam like the one and only time she had drunk withyweed ale, and the sheaf tumbled to the floor. She barely noticed, overwhelmed with her discovery.

'Kira?'

'I know what it is, Kest. I know what it is!' She gripped his arm. 'Come, we don't have much time.'

'Tell me what you're talking about!'

'Fireweed, Kest! It will cure Shargh wounds and it's in Kenclan octad. Come on!'

He stepped in front of her. 'Kenclan octad is a full day's travel, Kira, and we can't do it without food, and water, and rest, and we *won't* do it without a patrol.'

'We don't have time. We have to go *now*!'

She tried to duck around him, but he side-stepped. 'You don't have the right to risk yourself, even to save others. You carry all the Tremen's healing now.'

'We've had this stinking conversation before,' she exclaimed furiously. 'I'm not skulking in this hole while people die, even if you're prepared to.'

Kest's expression did not change but his hand fastened on her wrist, then he picked up the lamp, and dragged her from the cavern and back up the tunnel. Her father had done this to her, not by touch, but by intimidation. He had crushed and confined her for most of her life, and it was as if he were here now; his flesh as cold as the stone that pressed in upon her. She pulled in air, quicker and quicker but there was not enough, and the lamplight disappeared into dark blotches.

Kest heard her breathing change to a rapid pant, a sound he knew all too well. The younger Protectors had breathed like that during the attack on the Bough and, like them, Kira's gasps were caused by fear. He felt her crumple and managed to get his arm around her, set the lamp down, and lower her to the floor. Then he held her against him and pushed her head down between her knees. She felt fragile, like a bird. The mira kiraon; she was well-named, not just for her eyes but for her relentless hunting, in her case, of healing.

Kest shut his eyes wearily. He had never used force against a woman and now he had used it twice in a single day. But there was nothing in his Protector training that had taught him how to protect the most important person in Allogrenia, especially a person intent on throwing their life away.

She roused but remained slumped against him. 'I need to beg your pardon, Healer Kiraon,' he said formally. 'For now, and for what might come. You need to understand that I'm sworn to protect.' She turned and looked at him, so close that if he lowered his head now, he could kiss her. At least her face held no fear, and he was surprised by how much he *did not* want her to fear him.

'You're sworn to protect, Kest, and I am sworn to heal. I can't do what I've sworn to do, without your help. And you can't protect those of Allogrenia without *my* help. I have a map of the Warens. We can get to Kenclan octad from here. It will be quicker than going over-ground.'

Kest cursed silently. Did she never give up? She fumbled a page of Writings from inside her shirt and flattened it on the cavern floor. Her hands shook and Kest's regret deepened.

'There are three openings shown, see?' she said, and pointed to them. 'One in Renclan, and these two, that open in the Kenclan octad.'

46

Kest shifted the lamp closer. It was the most detailed map of the Warens he had ever seen. 'Where did you get this?'

'From the storeroom, before my oil ran out and you came.'

'And you never thought to tell me?' If there were maps like these in existence, the Warens could become a real part of Allogrenia's defences and not just a musty after-thought.

'I forgot about it. I'm sorry. But it means we can get to the Kenclan octad and back in a day.'

'What makes you think that?'

'Well, we are about here,' she said, her slender finger tracing the lines on the map. 'That's the Sarnia Room we've just been in. There's the Water Cavern and there are the training rooms. It's about half that distance again to this entrance.'

'You're assuming that it *is* an entrance, and that it *is* open, not blocked by rockfall, *and* that the map is to scale.'

'To *scale*?'

Kest pointed to the spaces between the caverns. 'That the distance here is, in fact, equal to the distance there.' Kira said nothing. 'And there is the little matter of an escort. You are *not* wandering about all over the octad looking for fireweed.'

'I won't be *wandering* about, Kest. It's on the slope directly beneath the Sarnia caves.'

'Oh, and you've only just remembered it?' He folded the map and helped her to her feet. 'This isn't a game, Kira; some competition about who gets their own way. The Shargh could be anywhere, and we already know their intentions.'

'Are you calling me a liar?' Her face had taken on all the petulance of Eser at her worst.

'I am saying it is strange that you suddenly have such precise knowledge.'

'You *are* calling me a liar!'

'Stop acting like a child!' he snapped. 'If you expect people to understand what's in your heart, you had better start telling them what's in your head.'

'I read of fireweed some time ago, *Commander,*' she clipped out. 'When we took the wounded to the Sarnia caves, I saw a herb I didn't recognize. You refused to give me time to examine it further. Just now I've read a description of fireweed's habits, and they match. Is that sufficient, *Commander*?'

'It's an improvement.'

'And will you help me or take me prisoner again?'

Stinking heart-rot! Why did she have to ask him such questions? Every shred of his Protector training told him it was madness to go to the Kenclan octad without a patrol. And neither of them had had food or rest for close to two days. The way he felt now, he would have trouble fighting off a stickspider. Yet if they went back to the training rooms to rest and eat *and* gather a patrol, the wounded would die; *his* men would die.

'We will go directly to the Sarnia caves. If there's no fireweed there, we will come straight back. No argument, no scouting about, no excuses. Do I have your word?'

'Yes.'

'And one last thing, Kira.' He bent, so that his face was level with hers. 'If we come under attack, at any time, you're to run and don't look back. Do you understand?' His eyes were hollow, his jaw shaded with stubble.

'I can't just leave you and—'

'*Do you understand*?'

She swallowed dryly. 'Yes.'

'Then let's go.'

6

The marwings circled higher and higher above the Grounds, their wings scarcely beating as they rode the hot air's back. Tarkenda came to a stop, shaded her eyes against the glare, and stared down at the dark blot on the bleached earth below.

Was it the putrefying corpse of an ebis that had given up the struggle to live, or a Shargh warrior returning from hunt? She wiped the wetness from her eyes and grunted in irritation. Maybe those the Sky Chiefs invited home early were blessed. They did not have to contend with rotted bones and clouded eyes.

She forced her aching hips into motion again up the spur. Arkendrin's fire circle remained empty and she did not need the sound of blackflies to know the remains of his food was devoured by things that stung and squirmed. It was fitting that the sorcha of a warrior who could not gift his brother even a single moon of mourning should become the haunt of lesser creatures. She wiped her eyes again and wondered how she had spawned such a son.

She did not know whether Arkendrin's nature had been seeded by his birth order or implanted by the Sky Chiefs while still in her belly. Even as a child he had secreted things away that should have been shared: the thickest wolf-skins and the season's first gathering of grahen eggs, and now he used his brother's mourning time to hunt the chiefship for himself.

She doubted Erboran would have acted so, had he been second-born. Erboran's love of the Shargh had gone beyond self-interest, and he had respected the Sky Chiefs' ways, and so kept the Shargh safe. There were many on the Grounds who were blind to his wisdom, and deaf to the tales of past suffering. They fed off Arkendrin's promises of future glory and in turn, Arkendrin fed off *them*.

A hot wind thudded the sorchas' hides against their struts and Tarkenda's lips thinned. Arkendrin had been born on such a day. Her sweat had mixed with her birth-waters on the bed as he had squalled, and Ergardrin had laughed as he had swung him, wet and bloodied, above Erboran's head. *Here I have a brother for you, little one, to test who might be chief.*

The words had chilled Tarkenda, but Ergardrin had dismissed her fears with a shrug, as he had dismissed her wanting of a daughter. *What is a daughter but a joining for some other man's son? There is plenty of time for daughters*, he had said. But there had been no time, and no daughters, just death and Arkendrin's hunger for the chiefship.

Erlken crouched at the front of Erboran's sorcha sharpening his flatsword. The whetstone rasped, and the blade caught the sun as he turned it. The dazzle filled Tarkenda's eyes and she saw the flash of many blades, the plunge and scream of horses, and the faces of fair-haired men. The vision was gone in a blink, and the thud of hoofs became the flap of sorchas again. Erlken still sharpened his flatsword and the marwings still circled overhead.

Tarkenda no longer questioned why the Sky Chiefs sent her visions while those around her remained untouched. Instead she spent her strength in struggle to understand them, and now effort held her motionless under the sun's beat and it was a moment before she became aware that Erlken squinted up at her, his hand to his forehead in respectful greeting.

51

'Where goes your father?' she asked.

'He didn't say, Chief-mother. Just asked me to be with the Chief-wife. She sleeps,' he added, as if to prove he'd not been remiss in his guarding. He grinned. His body was that of a man, but his face still held a boyish softness.

Tarkenda frowned. Ormadon had barely left Palansa's side since Erboran's death and must have good reason to do so now. She flicked open the door flap and was greeted with a wash of stifling air, thick with the scent of ripe cheese, ebis fleece, and burrel cones. She hobbled across the pelt-strewn floor, loosed a vent flap, and as a gust of warm air swept in, Palansa woke with a start.

'You would be dead now if I were an enemy,' said Tarkenda acidly.

'You would have had to kill Erlken first,' said Palansa, as she pushed the damp hair from her face.

Tarkenda poured herself a bowl of water and gulped it down. It was warm and mud-tainted. 'Simple enough,' she said, and wiped her mouth. 'Erlken lacks his father's fighting skills.'

Palansa rolled herself off the bed and came to the table. 'But he wouldn't die quietly, and I would have time to prepare.' She patted the dagger under her shirt. 'Arkendrin might kill me, but I would make sure he never became chief.'

Tarkenda's eyes hardened. 'There's no victory where you lose your own *and* your son's.' For a while the only sound was the flap of hides and creak of struts.

'Sometimes I hope the babe is a girl,' said Palansa dully, as she lowered herself onto a seat. 'Then we would both be safe.'

'Do you think Arkendrin would let his brother's seed live?' demanded Tarkenda. She poured Palansa a bowl of water and passed it to her. 'If the babe is a girl, then Arkendrin will be chief, and none will dare raise their voices against him, no matter what he did.'

Palansa's knuckles whitened on the bowl. 'Then I hope misfortune befalls him and he never returns!'

'Hope will serve us less well than action.'

Palansa said nothing and Tarkenda settled opposite. 'I've spread word of Arkendrin's breach of his brother's mourning time.'

'That won't dissuade his followers,' muttered Palansa. 'Even if he used Erboran's bones for blackfish bait, they'd still lick at his heels, waiting for *his* fortunes to drag *theirs* up the spur.' She wandered back to the bed and picked up the part-finished keep-pot she had been weaving when sleep had overtaken her.

'The wolf chases only what it can catch,' said Tarkenda. 'We won't waste our strength on those who have already tied their futures to Arkendrin's. We must focus on those who waver, on those who wait to see which way things turn.'

Palansa traced the pattern of flatswords she had worked into the pot's side. 'What if Arkendrin brings the gold-eyed Healer back?'

'I don't think he will.'

'Do you doubt his hunting skills?'

'The Sky Chiefs have sent me more visions,' said Tarkenda grimly.

The pot dropped from Palansa's hands. 'You know my son will be safe?'

Tarkenda sighed. 'Do you think if I knew that I would have kept it from you? Do you think Ormadon would be

53

like a shadow at your back?' She poured herself another bowl of water and drank it despite its taint. Her mouth was drier than a beetle husk.

'Then what . . .?'

'I have seen fighting.'

'That could mean anything.'

'Fair men on white horses,' said Tarkenda slowly.

'Northerners,' hissed Palansa.

Tarkenda went back to the door and pushed the flap wide. She felt suffocated, as if the sorcha held insufficient air. 'It may be that I see echoes of old visions, of things already passed.' She peered across the Grounds, instinctively searching for anything amiss, and Palansa came to her side.

'Do you believe that?' she asked. Her hand had crept to the dagger under her shirt.

'No.' Tarkenda let the door flap fall. 'I think what I see is yet to come. The Last Telling speaks of horses in the south-west.'

'*If horses graze in forests deep.*'

Tarkenda whirled. 'You know the Telling?'

'I . . . I asked Erboran for it. I told him I should know what our son must carry forward.'

Tarkenda winced as she lowered herself onto her seat. 'And what did Erboran say to that? We both know the Last Telling isn't shared.'

'He said I was a troublesome woman who gave him no peace.' Palansa smiled but her eyes glistened with tears.

'Yet he told you, as Ergardrin told me,' said Tarkenda. 'Perhaps they sensed they wouldn't live to raise their sons.'

'Northerners fighting us,' murmured Palansa. 'It makes no sense given they've ignored us since we've stayed south of the Braghans. Maybe the horses of the Telling are Ashmiri.'

'The Last Telling has naught to do with the Ashmiri,' said Tarkenda dismissively.

Palansa's brows drew in an intense frown. 'But why would the Northerners go all the way to the south-western forests? The part about the horses comes later too, which suggests the first part of the Telling has already unfolded and the Healer *has* seen the sun set. And if that happened, it means Arkendrin would have failed.'

'Not necessarily. Arkendrin might kill her *after* she leaves the forest.' Tarkenda shrugged. 'Assuming the Healer of the Last Telling *is* the Healer of the forest, and the gold *is* the gold of her eyes. The Sky Chiefs aren't renowned for the clarity of their sendings. It might also mean that Arkendrin has taken us north, beyond the Braghans, as he's long wanted to do. Then there *would* be fighting. The Northerners won't tolerate us on *their* plains.'

'There would be much blood spilled,' said Palansa grimly, 'and the Telling hints it would be ours, not theirs, because our flatswords will fail.'

'*Fire will be the flatsword's bane and bring the dead to life again,*' quoted Tarkenda.

'How can fire destroy flatswords other than by melting them?' demanded Palansa. 'Was there fire in your visions?'

'Yes, but what the Sky Chiefs send is not like the view over the Grounds, but fragments of this and that, flowing together like weed under water.'

'It's strange the Sky Chiefs favor you in this way,' said Palansa. 'Perhaps they aid us, intending my son to be chief.'

'I am not sure it's aid they send,' said Tarkenda. She had seen enough seasons come and go to know the Sky Chiefs favored no one, but she did not want to crush Palansa's hope. She remembered all too well how important hope had been in the long nights following Ergardrin's death. 'Did Ormadon tell you Arkendrin's taken Irason south-west?' she asked. Palansa nodded. 'No doubt he intends to use him to speak to one of the treemen.'

'The treemen will be on their guard now and unlikely to wander alone in the trees,' pointed out Palansa. She rose and rubbed her back. 'Arkendrin will have trouble finding the Healer, and that bodes well for us.'

Tarkenda's fingers drummed the table. 'I don't think any of it bodes well,' she admitted. 'Spilled blood has a habit of drawing more.' Her shrewd gaze fixed on Palansa. 'Have you heard tell of how Erboran died?'

'No,' said Palansa thickly. 'Only Arkendrin's braggings about his own *valiant* efforts.'

'You would think it would be simple to kill a single, unarmed girl, wouldn't you? Yet Erboran is dead and she lives.'

Palansa stiffened. 'What are you saying?'

'That the Last Telling might be a warning.'

'Of course, it's a warning. The Healer mustn't be allowed to see a setting sun, or else the rest of the Telling will unfold.'

'Or we will *cause* it to unfold.'

'You speak in riddles,' said Palansa irritably, settling on the seat again.

'Arkendrin boasts that Erboran's death was avenged by the deaths of many treemen, and that he slew all who had stood with the Healer-creature at their wooden sorcha,' said Tarkenda. 'The Healer might flee the trees to escape us.'

'You think the Sky Chiefs have tricked us?'

'It's not for us to judge the Sky Chiefs,' said Tarkenda, with sudden solemnity, 'nor to question the moons of honoring owed to those who have passed into their realm.'

'You will seed the sorchas with the idea that the Telling can be read two ways?' pursued Palansa, not put off by Tarkenda's change of tack.

Tarkenda eyed her approvingly; Erboran had chosen his join-wife well. 'I think it's time you called a Speak. Such an important possibility needs to be debated.'

'And the warriors need to be reminded of the importance of honoring the dead,' said Palansa. 'We can hardly expect the Sky Chiefs to lend us the wisdom to fathom their Tellings, if we withhold the respect owed to them.'

'Yes,' said Tarkenda. 'It would be good to remind the likes of Irdodun and Urpalin that there is a cost to running at Arkendrin's heels.'

7

Kest stopped and held the map up to the lamp. 'We should have been out by now,' he said, and cursed under his breath. 'I'm beginning to think this map isn't accurate.'

Kira had to resist the temptation to sit down fearing she would not get up again. 'It shows the training rooms and the Water Cavern in the right places,' she said dully, '*and* the Sarnia Room.' Even speaking was an effort.

'Then it mustn't be to scale. We should have come to the opening by now.' Kest stared back the way they had come. 'Unless we've missed it.'

'We haven't missed it, Kest.'

'How can you be so certain?'

'We have a lamp and two sets of eyes.' Kest grimaced and folded the map. 'It can't be much further,' said Kira, and started off again. 'I hope,' she muttered. She trudged on and the tunnel floor started to climb, imperceptibly at first, and then more steeply. 'It must be ending,' she called over her shoulder.

'Keep your voice down,' warned Kest, and hurried after her. 'And don't get too far ahead.'

Kira slowed her pace, but her thoughts ran on. Once she had the fireweed, they would need to get back to the training rooms as swiftly as possible. It would probably be best applied as a paste directly onto the wound. The sheaf had described the fireweed as highly potent, so she would not need much. Then her eyes widened, and she stopped.

'What—' exclaimed Kest in irritation, as he all but cannoned into her, then saw what she had seen. 'Stinking heart-rot!'

The tunnel split, with one branch going left and the other turning sharply right. 'Look at the map,' said Kira.

'I don't need to. It doesn't show any stinking junction.' Kira stared at the walls but there was no soot, or brackets for lamps, or markings of any kind to show which way to go. 'Shall we toss a stone and see whether it lands smooth or rough side up?' suggested Kest sourly.

'We take the tunnel on the right,' said Kira.

'Why the right?'

Kira sighed. 'The first entrance was easterly, remember?'

'The tunnel might loop back west, or south, or north for all we know.'

'Well let's find out.'

Kira strode off with more confidence than she felt, but the tunnel twisted back on itself and her heart sank. For want of a better alternative, she kept going, and after a while it swung east again and started to climb. 'It looks like—' she began and froze, as she heard a noise like metal on metal.

'What is it?' hissed Kest behind her and drew his sword.

'Did you hear that?' Kest shook his head and Kira's heart pounded. It was quiet now. They stood straining into the darkness but still there was nothing, and Kira was about to suggest they went on when it sounded again. Kest thrust Kira behind him and her heart thundered, drowning all thought. The noise sounded oddly familiar and she breathed again. 'I think it's birds,' she whispered.

'No bird sounds like that!'

'I think the stone's distorting the sound.'

'Wait here,' said Kest. He set the lamp down and crept forward, the gleam of his sword the last thing Kira saw before the darkness swallowed that too.

Silence closed in and Kira started to pace. She was weary but doing nothing was impossible. What if Kest did not return? What if the Shargh lay in wait? Kest might already be dead and the Shargh creeping back down the tunnel. Her scalp prickled and she imagined she could hear stealthy footsteps.

Then she *could* hear stealthy footsteps! She snatched up the lamp and drew her arm back. Hot oil in their faces should give her a few moments before their blades plunged into her back. She sucked in her breath, braced herself and then Kest emerged from the murk, and Kira gave a choking cry and collapsed into his arms. 'Kira! What is it?' he asked in alarm.

'I thought . . .' She shook, and the tremors made speech difficult. 'I thought . . .' she began again but got no further and buried her face in his shirt. He smelled of sweat and dust and burned espin, but she heard the reassuring thud of his heart, and his arms tightened round her, calming her. 'I thought you were dead,' she mumbled, as she stepped back and concentrated on smoothing her crumpled shirt.

He smiled. 'Pecked to death by a nest of tippets. You were right, the stone here *does* do strange things to sound. The entrance can't be very far ahead. We need take care. Come.' He took her hand, for which she was grateful, and the light grew as they went forward. The stone went from black to brown, then to grey, as it was lit by the silvery sheen of dusk.

The noise resolved itself too, into the chirp of tippets, and then the cries of springleslips, honeysprites and leaf

60

thrushes intruded, and the air took on the myriad scents of the forest. But instead of an exit like the one guarded by Nogren, the tunnel ended in a wall of tumbled rocks.

There was a small opening above, and Kest held the lamp aloft to illuminate the pale sun-starved tendrils of a sour-ripe vine that cascaded into the tunnel. He swore as he stared up at it. 'We've come all this stinking way for nothing.'

'I can fit through it,' said Kira.

'No!'

'Kest . . .'

'Absolutely not! I forbid it.'

'We agreed you wouldn't hold me prisoner again.'

'We agreed we would stay together!' His hands came to his hips. 'You're asking me to break *every* tenet of Protector training, to toss aside *every* rule I've obeyed for eight seasons *and* forced my men to obey on pain of incarceration! I can't do it, Kira. I *won't* do it!'

Kest's face was haggard, his eyes dark with exhaustion. They were the same, Kira realized abruptly. Kest needed to protect in the same way that she needed to heal. The revelation comforted her, and she laid her hand on his arm. 'Kasheron never intended Protecting and healing to fight each other, but to work together to make the Tremen strong. Most of the wounded in the training rooms are Protectors, Kest. Kesilini lives because of them, *I* live because of them. They did what they were trained to do. Now let me do what I am trained to do.'

'Don't ask me to do this, Kira.'

The anguish in his voice was clear and there was a long silence. 'I need your help to reach the opening, Kest.'

He shook his head. 'How did you get to be so cursed stubborn?'

His voice was ragged and she made a determined effort to lighten hers. 'Perhaps it's the company I've been keeping lately.'

He did not smile. 'Our agreement stands. You go straight there and come straight back. If there's no fireweed, you don't look for it *and*, you don't leave until it is dark.'

Kira nodded. 'It's almost dark now. Give me a leg up.'

'Wait,' said Kest, and drew his sword. 'I'll clear the sour-ripe.'

'No. It's better the opening stays hidden,' she said. 'A few scratches won't kill me.'

'But the Shargh will.' His warm hands cupped her face and forced her eyes to meet his. 'You have no love for yourself, Kira, but you are loved by many. Remember that.'

Kira nodded, her throat too tight to speak. Then Kest linked his hands and she placed her foot in them. It brought their faces close together. 'Take very great care, Kira.'

She nodded again, and he hefted her skyward. She grabbed the edge of the opening and got her heel onto the stone. The sour-ripe dragged her back, as if it resented her exit, but she wedged her shoulders through its tangle and scrabbled clear of its rip and tear into the leaf-litter. Her hands were horribly scratched but she had kept the worst of it off her face, and there was a major compensation for her pain and effort: the sour-ripe was loaded with fruit.

'A fair trade,' she muttered, as she stuffed her mouth and filled her pockets. 'Your flesh for mine.' She ate greedily, the sweet juices slaking her thirst and sating her empty belly, and then crawled back to the opening and called softly to Kest.

'Yes?'

'Catch.' There was an exclamation and a muffled chuckle. 'I'll get you some more when I come back.'

'Be swift,' he whispered, but she was already gone.

Kest lowered himself back onto the dusty floor and quenched the lamp to save oil. It was completely dark outside now, the opening's edges limned by star sheen and light from the waning moon. It would be a good time to get some sleep, but he was haunted by having let her go.

Kasheron's dream of a place of healing, built through seasons of struggle and sacrifice, and the slow recording of healing herbs, now rested in the memory of a single person, that he, Kest of Morclan, *would-be Protector Commander*, had sent off *alone* into a forest where Shargh might lurk.

He rested his head back against the stone and shut his eyes. Yet what alternative did he have? Backtrack until they found the second opening? If there *were* one. Force Kira back to watch the wounded die, like he had intended? He sighed. There was no point in fretting. For good or ill, she was gone, and he must wait for what was to come, whether it be good, or the ending of everything Kasheron had dreamed of.

Kira ran, spurred on by desperation and fear. Speed was now the only thing that would save those in the Haelen, but fear was like an animal at her throat. She kept to the darkest blots of shadow and avoided the snap and crack of windfall as she fought to trick her body that the pain in her legs and chest did not exist. If she were right in her reckoning, and *if* the opening to the Warens *was* where she thought it was, then the lands that bordered the Sarnia caves should be close-by. *Should be*! Yet she recognized nothing.

The litter near the Sarnia caves had been dry and thick but here it barely covered the simpleweed. Maybe the tunnel opening she had scrambled through was not in Kenclan at all; maybe the map was completely wrong. Panic threatened, and she scanned frantically but could see nothing beyond the wall of trees. She needed higher ground to orientate herself.

She started up the slope and stopped as she recalled that white stone had poked from the ground near the cave, and even with a waning moon, it should be visible, but the ground was dark. It might be on the next slope *or* she might be completely lost. She gritted her teeth and forced her trembling legs down into the shallow valley and up the other side. She had to stop more than once to catch her breath, and when she reached the next crest, rewarded herself with the last of the sour-ripe.

A bitterberry bush thrashed sideways as a leaf-thrush winged away and she stifled a scream. Leaves whispered around her and scuttles in the undergrowth took on the sounds of hunting footsteps. She had to fight the urge to look over her shoulder every second step.

She crept on, straining into the gloom, and saw something glimmer on the next slope. Micklefungus or stone? She struggled down through the bitterberry and up the other side and the rich smell of leaf-fall quickened her heart. The glimmer turned out to be stone and the contorted sever tree to her right looked familiar too, as did the stand of shelterbush.

She picked her way carefully up between the stones, the litter so thick it reached her ankles, and stopped, her mind suddenly as blank as the night around her. The memory she had boasted of to Kest, had gone. A part of her knew it was probably exhaustion, but panic threatened.

She stood trembling, while sweat oozed down her back and then, more by instinct than anything else, turned back and, as the leaf litter deepened, dropped to her knees, and raked her hands through it. Nothing. She groveled forward, ignoring the jab of a stick in her calf, and the possibility of trawling up a stickspider, but still there was nothing.

Sweat stung her eyes and she blinked ferociously. It *must* be here! Her fingers stabbed into slime and she recoiled in disgust. It did not make sense, *unless* there were small soaks hidden amongst the stone. Her heart quickened. It would explain the withyweed she had seen with Kest's patrol too.

She quelled the surge of hope and crawled forward, and then her left hand connected with something spongy, and she pushed aside the litter to expose a row of fingers. The smaller ones were pale and the larger ones dark-tipped. Kira gave a sob of relief, the Writing clear in her mind: *the fireweed darkens to a deep red at maturity when its potency is greatest.*

Her hands shook as she retrieved her herbing sickle and harvested. The larger fingers came away cleanly as if they were ripe, and as she had no herbal sling, she laid them gently inside her shirt. They grew in a run, and she followed the trail, smoothing away the leaf-fall, harvesting, and reburying the immature plants.

She had collected more than a dozen ripe fingers before the run ended but she did not know if it would be enough. The Writings had said nothing about quantities or how best to store it, but she had read of its potency more than once and her Healer sensitivities rebelled against wasting it.

She stowed the sickle and rose, and then, a figure loomed from the shadows. Her brain screamed at her to run but her legs refused to move. The figure drew closer, but still she remained rooted to the spot, barely able to breathe. 'I greet you, clansman,' the figure said.

It was the customary greeting of one Tremen stranger to another. Kira's mouth formed a word, but nothing came out. He was little more than a boy, she noticed dazedly, despite his height. 'I . . . I am sorry, Healer Kiraon, I didn't recognize you in the dark.'

'You startled me,' she finally choked. More like scared the life out of her! She dragged in some air. 'I didn't expect to see a Kenclansman beyond the First Eight.'

'I'm not a Kenclansman, I am Bern of Sherclan,' he said proudly.

'A Sherclansman? You're a long way from your longhouse, Bern. Doesn't Clanleader Dakresh forbid such journeys?'

'Clanleader Dakresh believes the danger of another attack before the full moon is small, and I agree with him. He is happy enough for us to journey until the moon is bigger.'

'Anywhere? Or just within your own octad?' asked Kira shrewdly.

Bern shrugged, his eyes on the ground. 'I know every stand of shelterbush and clump of simpleweed in my octad, *and* in Barclan's octad, but it's different here. There are caves.' Kest believed the threat of attack was real, regardless of the moon's size, but she did not have the authority to order Bern home.

66

'Have you been to caves?' he asked excitedly. 'They are massive, with white stone that goes on forever.' He grinned. 'One of them even has water under it. I've slept there. and you can hear it through the stone.' His excitement reminded her of Kandor and of her own delight in wandering, but Kest was not a fool.

'The Protectors prefer people don't journey on their own, especially outside the First Eight. It would be safer if you returned to your longhouse.'

'You're journeying alone,' he pointed out.

'I'm gathering.'

There was an uncomfortable silence. 'I just want to spend a couple of nights at the caves, that's all,' said Bern. 'Then I'll go home.' He paused. 'You won't tell the Protectors you've seen me, will you?'

'Why? Have you disobeyed their orders?' she asked, noticing his bulging pack for the first time.

'No, my father's.'

'Your father's?'

'Dakresh.'

'*Clanleader* Dakresh?' asked Kira in astonishment. Bern nodded. Miken had once described Dakresh as a man as stuck in his ways as a root through rock, and he was old. Kira was surprised he had a son as young as Bern. Maybe he had bonded more than once. It was said Sherclan changed their bondmates more often than the withysnake its skin.

Bern waited anxiously, and she thought of her own father's prohibitions. 'I'm living in the Warens at the moment, and unlikely to see your father in the next few days. As long as you're back in your longhouse by then, I see no reason to mention seeing you.'

He grinned, and with a clumsy bow, bounded off up the slope. If only her legs would carry her as fast, she thought dourly, as she set off in the opposite direction. She searched for landmarks as she went. There were the twin-crowned castellas, here the tangle of shaggyman that clung to the bough next to the micklefungus. She passed the sequence of shelterbush and bitterberry next, her progress tortuously slow. She knew she should run but even walking took every last part of strength. She trudged on.

8

Springleslips greeted the dawn before Kira reached the sour-ripe covered hole, and she numbly filled her pockets with fruit, and hissed Kest's name. She was too tired to wait for a reply, just shoved her feet through the opening, folded her arms around her face, and dropped.

There was a grunted oath as Kest caught her and she was crushed against the comforting smell of his jacket. For a long moment he simply held her. 'Praise to the alwaysgreen which Shelters us,' he muttered. 'You took long enough.'

It was dark in the cave after the dawn-lit forest and Kira could barely make out his face. 'Did you run out of oil?' she asked.

'I'm saving it.' Flints scraped, and the burst of lamplight revealed Kest's haggardness with shocking clarity. He looked as if he had not slept in days, and Kira's heart faltered. Kest was no longer the aloof Protector she had first met near Nogren, nor the one who had held her to his will on the nightmarish journey to and from the Sarnia caves.

He was the companion who had run with her through the rain-filled night in the quest for sorren; who had searched in the darkness with her for Writings on fireweed; the friend who had just hugged her in relief at her safe return.

And she had seen the other side of him too, his head thrown back in joyous laughter as he had danced with her in the Morclan longhouse after the birth of Feseren's son. He was her bond-brother as well, and she wanted to tell

69

him how much he meant to her. 'You should have rested while I was away,' she blurted, and bit her lip, aware it sounded like a criticism.

Kest was busy packing away the flints. 'Rested? With you out there with the 'green knows how many stinking Shargh.' He cleared his throat and when he straightened, his face was expressionless. 'You *did* get the fireweed?' he asked, as they walked. Kira patted her shirt.
'And with no trouble?'

'It took me a while to find it. I don't seem to know Kenclan octad as well as I thought.' Kira's face warmed, but Kest hadn't actually asked her if she had seen anyone else.

'Was there much there?'

'Enough for two more harvests,' said Kira thickly, as her exhaustion returned with crushing suddenness.

'Only two?'

'The Writings say it's potent and I didn't search for more,' she mumbled. Even speaking had become an effort. 'Now I know its habit, I might be able to harvest it closer to the Bou—training room.'

'Or the Protectors will.'

Kira did not argue. The lamplight had blurred giving her the illusion that she walked in a yellow bubble. They went in silence and finally passed the gaping mouth of a large cavern. 'The storage room,' croaked Kest.

Kira nodded. How much further? And when she got back, how much longer before she could sleep? The Writing had said nothing of fireweed's preparation. It was probably recorded elsewhere but there had been no time to search. No time, no time, no time. She stumbled and only Kest's quick reflexes stopped her crashing to the floor. His hand remained on her arm and she wondered whether it was possible to sleep and walk at the same.

At some point Kest's grip shifted to her waist, and she leaned against him, comforted by his strength. He all but carried her but she was too tired to even thank him. Finally, as if in a dream, the darkness dissipated, and she became aware of Tresen, Miken, and Kesilini. 'We've found something that might cure Shargh wounds,' she mumbled. Tresen gave a yelp of excitement. 'It's the fireweed I told you about, before . . .' Kira slurred to a stop and extricated it from her shirt.

'It looks more like fungus than weed,' said Tresen, turning it over curiously.

'But how—' began Miken.

'Make a paste,' said Kira, the last of her strength focused on Tresen.

'What makes you think—' tried Miken again.

'I'll need bandages, Tresen.' She paused. 'How much sickleseed's left?'

'Kesilini made up two pots last night, but I'm not sure how much leaf is still there.'

'Wait for me,' she said, and staggering off to her alcove.

Miken turned back to Tresen, but he already headed for the Herbery, and that left Kest who was now being supported rather than embraced by Kesilini. There was much Miken needed to say, *and* to know, but again it seemed he would have to wait.

Kira collapsed onto her mattress and dragged her pack onto her lap. The pouch was double wrapped and had been in her pack since last summer. She tipped the hard, glossy seeds into her hand. Morning-bright: the leaves gave the training rooms their pleasant smell, but its seeds were poisonous, or so the Tremen believed.

Kira rolled them back and forth in her palm. The Writings said those of the north who took morning-bright seeds ran and fought for days, sometimes until their hearts stopped, and then they had dropped where they had stood.

She did not want to run or fight, just to heal, and would only take one little seed, so surely the effects shouldn't be as punishing? A groan sounded from beyond the curtain and she screwed her eyes shut, placed a seed on her tongue, and swallowed. The effect was immediate, as if she had swallowed a fire-spark.

She heaved herself up and gulped down a cup of water, but far from quenching the fire, it seemed to add fuel. Heat speared through her chest and arms and she coughed violently, dragged in air, and as the heat redoubled, sweat poured from her skin. Her brain felt like a furnace fit to explode and then, as suddenly as it had started, the heat drained away and she sagged backwards gasping.

Thank the 'green she felt normal again, well not exactly normal. Nothing ached or begged for rest, and the crushing exhaustion had gone. She changed into fresh clothes from the pile on the mattress and scrubbed her face and hands. Two more days, she promised herself, as she stowed the seeds safely away, then she would rest.

Tresen had returned and unbound Fedren's wound, and he looked up in surprise. 'You should be sleeping,' he said. 'You must be exhausted.' He had ground the fireweed and a bowl of pinkish red paste sat ready, yet she hesitated. What did she *really* know about fireweed apart from Writings made by those who shared the Terak Kutan's blood?

'Werrem and I can heal,' he said, his gaze sharp on her. Werrem hovered behind Tresen with a supply of fresh bandages but Kira shook her head. 'Well, if you insist on healing yourself, don't delay,' he snapped.

She ladled the paste onto Fedren's wound so that it covered every part of the raw, rancid flesh, then moved onto Berik, while behind her, Tresen bound Fedren again. She wondered whether Fedren would die anyway, or worse still, die an agonizing death, and her hands stilled. 'Maybe we should wait,' she said slowly.

'For what? Death?' demanded Tresen. 'Don't hold me up, Kira. I'm almost finished here.'

Kira reluctantly lathed paste into Berik's wound and moved on to old Miren. Next to him lay his grandson, his face as pale as wax, then Narek, Pirten, Sorosen, Dorn, and Firgen, then those with lesser wounds. She toiled on in silence, lost in the ghastly rhythm of stripping away oozing bandages and lathing stinking flesh. Finally, she came to the last of the wounded, sat back on her heels, and put the bowl aside.

She heard the chink of chimes but it took her a moment to realize it was impossible, because the Warens lacked wind. It was the chink of cups, she realized dully. Kesilini had returned and set one of the side tables with thornyflower tea, and plates of nutbread.

'Come and eat, Kira,' she said. 'Then you must rest.'

Kira scrubbed her hands in a wash bowl and settled at the table. It must be close to midday, but she felt no cramps from kneeling, or aches from bending. She watched Kesilini pour the tea, but it was as if she watched her from afar. Kesilini's likeness to her brother was startling. She had the same white-blonde hair and the same blue eyes, now clearly puzzled. 'I don't understand how you're still healing when Kest sleeps as if dead,' she murmured.

'It's because she has taken something,' said Tresen, as he pulled his chair alongside. His face was as hard as his voice.

'Taken something?' said Kesilini.

'*Good* Healers know the green and growing gives us herbs that mend flesh and knit bones,' he said, his gaze on Kira unwavering. 'And that it also gives us herbs that make flight seem possible or even bring death. *Good* Healers don't misuse their knowing.'

Kira's head came up. 'I didn't have any choice.'

'Of course you had a choice! Why do you always think you have to do *everything* on your own? I could have lathed the wounds and Kesilini could have bound them, and there's Arlen and Paterek as well as Werem. Who do you think healed while you were away wandering in the Warens?'

Anger roared, as explosive as it was unexpected, and Kira slammed her cup down, scalding her fingers. '*I* gave them the fireweed! *I* gave them something we know nothing about! It's *my* task to mend what might come of it, this night, or tomorrow, or the day after!'

'The day after? What in the 'green have you taken?' He caught her wrist and his expression turned to horror.

'What is it? What's wrong?' asked Kesilini tremulously.

Tresen's voice was sharp with fear. 'Your heart's thrashing like the Drinkwater in flood! Do you know what you're risking?'

Kira snatched her hand back and shoved her chair from the table. 'It's nothing to do with you!' There was a shuddering groan and she spun. 'Who?'

74

Tresen was on his feet too. 'I didn't see . . .'

'Serdric, I think,' said Kesilini.

Serdric was one of the last Kira had treated, and his head now tossed from side to side. Kira hastened to him. His skin was florid and slick with sweat. 'He is burning!' she exclaimed. She felt for his pulse and his arm flailed, dealing her a stinging blow to the face, and knocking her backwards. Another groan erupted from the far side of the room and Kira scrambled upright and looked around wildly.

'Maybe we shouldn't have treated them all at once,' said Tresen, as he struggled to restrain another tossing man, while a choking sound began behind him.

'It's made them worse,' exclaimed Kesilini.

'Fetch all the sickleseed we have,' ordered Tresen, '*and* the other Healers. We're going to need everyone.'

Tresen had no idea how long it was before the screams and thrashings gave way to the quiet of uneasy sleep. All he knew was he never wanted to endure anything like that again. Fireweed had certainly burned the rot from their wounds, but it had brought with it a ferocious fever barbed with a pain so severe that even sickleseed failed to dull it. And it had come too late for Miren and his grandson.

He glared at Kira, still bent in tending. He did not know what angered him most: her abuse of herbs or her refusal to acknowledge doing so. It was as if she had closed off; as if all their time growing together had never existed.

A hand gripped his shoulder and he jumped. 'I hear I missed some very strange happenings,' said Miken.

'Giving a room full of wounded men a fever-bringing herb at exactly the same time is probably not a good idea,' conceded Tresen.

'But it worked?'

Tresen nodded and his father's grip tightened, bringing home to Tresen the enormity of their achievement. They had cured Shargh wounds!

'It's spoken of throughout the Warens but I hardly dared believe it true,' said Miken. 'This is a great day for the Tremen.'

'But not for Kira.'

Miken's smile drained away. 'Tell me.'

Kira blinked as the wavering form of Miken picked his way through the wounded towards her. He looked as though he swam under water and she resisted the urge to giggle. He took her arm and lifted her. 'Come,' he said, guiding her back to her alcove. He flicked back the bed cover. 'Lie down.'

The mattress moved like water too, but she obediently lay down, and Miken took off her boots and pulled the cover over her. 'What have you taken?' he asked.

'Morning-bright.'

'I thought it was poisonous.' He brought his hand to her neck, then Kira watched him float away and float back. He pushed a rough sack of some herb under her legs. 'That will take some of the strain off your heart,' he said. 'You're to stay like that until I tell you otherwise.' Wood scraped against stone as he settled on a chair. 'How do you feel?'

'Like my head is at the First Eight.'

Miken grunted. 'Anything else?'

'I'm having trouble seeing.'

'What about your hearing?'

'I can hear.'

'Good, because I'm going to talk, and you're going to listen. The council has appointed you Tremen Leader, and Kest, Protector Commander. I think they've chosen well on both counts.'

Kira felt like protesting, but the cover was warm and Miken's blurry outline had given way to blackness. 'I have never wanted the leadership,' she managed to say.

'I know, but the best Healer in Allogrenia becomes its leader, and you've long been that. Your role will not be greatly different to what you do now. You will continue to heal and keep healing-knowing safe, while Kest will ensure the protection of the Tremen. Neither of you will do these things alone. You will have the support and help of the council, and of all who dwell in Allogrenia.'

Kira said nothing and felt Miken's hand on her neck once more. 'I think your heart has slowed. Do you feel calmer?' he asked.

'I'm tired.'

Rough fingers smoothed the hair back from her face. He had stroked her hair like this when she was a child, comforting her after her mother's death, and as she grew, as he had healed her small hurts, or held her as she wept. 'I have something for you,' he said, and Kira felt a smooth cylinder of wood put into her hands.

'It's Kandor's pipe,' he said gently.

The darkness became a sleet-storm. 'I don't want it.'

Miken's warm hands closed over hers. 'Remember his smile, Kira, and his love of music, and his love for you.' Miken's voice whispered like the wind through the canopy and his lips brushed her forehead. 'Sleep now, dear one.'

His words slipped away into nothingness and Kira tightened her grip on the pipe. Tears wet her face. At least she could still feel, she thought vaguely, and then that sense was swallowed too.

9

Arkendrin cursed as he flicked the flies away. They might be smaller than the blackflies of the Grounds, but they were just as thick, and just as greedy as they fed off the mess that coated the broken bushes. The treeman screamed and sobbed, and bucked under Ermashin's grip, and his trousers were dark where he had wet himself. Arkendrin's lip curled. The treeman might be tall but he squalled like a babe denied the teat.

Urpalin slid his dagger over the treeman's shoulder to tease him before he sliced again. The treeman shrieked and his gurglings formed the word they already knew meant owl. 'I need more than *owl*,' snarled Arkendrin, and he needed it now. Palansa's belly swelled with each passing day and the waverers on the Grounds swayed more in her filthy direction.

The Sky Chiefs had granted him the creature's name earlier and now he knew its meaning, but he was still no closer to destroying the cursed creature. 'Find out where the *Kiraon-owl* is,' he ordered.

Irason leaned forward again but his belly heaved at the stench of blood. The day was hot and he had waited a long time under the trees for Arkendrin to bring the treeman. He was very thirsty but Arkendrin had offered him no water and he daren't ask for any. His head swam and he wobbled, almost toppling onto the blood-soaked treeman.

Orthakin steadied him and Irason searched desperately for more northern words. 'Is *Kiraon-owl* where?' he said carefully. The treeman's eyes were unfocused and Irason doubted the treeman heard him. 'Where is *Kiraon-owl*?' he tried again, wondering if a different word order helped.

Urpalin raised his dagger again and Irason had to clench his teeth to stop their rattle. The treeman screamed a new word. '*Warens*,' said Irason tentatively. The word was strange to him. '*Warens*,' he repeated, and looked at Arkendrin.

'What *are* these cursed *warens*?' demanded Arkendrin, his hand going to his sword.

Irason wiped his sweaty brow and turned back to the treeman. '*Warens* where place *Kiraon-owl* is?'

The treeman panted now, his sobs reduced to harsh whimpers, and Irason wondered if he were dying. The treeman's shirt was sodden and rivulets of blood pooled to either side of him. Irason glanced at Ermashin, but Ermashin's face was blank, unlike Arkendrin's, which was like thunder. He drew his flatsword. 'What is *warens*?' he bawled.

Irason cringed and Urpalin's lips drew back in a snarl as he brought the knife down again. Blood spurted from the treeman's neck, wetting Irason, and the treeman gurgled a single word and convulsed. '*Hole*,' croaked Irason, before his belly emptied itself onto the grass. Orthaken steadied him again him until his retching quieted and he became aware the treeman was quiet too. He wiped his mouth and looked up in time to see Arkendrin's fist send Urpalin sprawling.

Arkendrin's sword reduced the surrounding bushes to shreds. Three stinking days of following slashed trees! Three more stumbling about in the murk in search of a treeman! Another three dragging him to the forest's edge! And all wasted because Urpalin did not know the difference between pain and death. He cursed savagely.

The first gave information, the second nothing! All they had discovered for their trouble was the creature's name meant owl and that it lived in a hole. A hole! Surely Irason was mistaken? Arkendrin glared at the old man crouched next to his blood-tie and he seemed to shrivel.

He cursed again. He would delay no longer in this filthy tangle! He thrust his sword into his belt, heaved on his pack, and strode off through the trees.

Kira drew the fragrant air deep into her lungs. Never had the forest looked so beautiful or smelled so wonderful. Everything was scent-drenched and sun-dappled, with glittering columns of flutterwings spiraling from the forest floor and flowerthieves chattering high in the sever trees. *This* was where she needed to be, not in the Warens!

But she was no longer just a Healer, free to wander at will. She was the Tremen Leader, off to her first Clancouncil to confront the clanleaders, half of whom did o't want her. She glanced at the Protectors who walked nearby, and at those who slipped through the trees, and surreptitiously hitched up her leggings. They were too big, as was her tunic.

She'd had to roll up the sleeves, hiding some of their beautiful embroidery. It was of alwaysgreen leaves, the mark of Kashclan, and the clothes were Tenerini's. Miken had told her Tenerini was busy with her needle making Kira new clothing, but it was not ready and so Tenerini had sent her own for Kira to wear at her first council. Miken was proud the new Tremen Leader was Kashclan, but Kira wondered whether she would make such a mess of it, his pride would turn to shame.

She snapped off a twig of sweetchew and concentrated on removing the bark. It finally slipped off and she popped the sweetchew into her mouth. Tresen loved sweetchew. *As sweet as honey*, he said. *Sweeter than honey*, Kandor had always retorted. She stumbled, and a Protector caught her arm. 'Please take care, Leader Feailner Kiraon.'

'I . . . I will, thank you. And I'm just Leader Kiraon.'

The Protector was an older man Kira did not recognize, and one who was now clearly puzzled. 'Your pardon, Leader Kiraon. It's many seasons since we've had the honor of a female leader, and Commander Kest himself instructed us on how to address you.'

Kest obviously wanted her ability to take pain recognized, despite his pledge not to speak of it, and Kira took out her irritation on another twig of sweetchew. He probably meant well, she conceded as her ill temper eased, and the last thing she wanted was to undermine his authority. 'Commander Kest is correct,' she said carefully, 'but I don't think we need to remind the Tremen that I'm a woman by including *feailner* in my title.'

The Protector gave a small bow. 'As you wish, Leader Kiraon.'

They went on, the only sound the soft thud of their footsteps and the calls of the tippets as they joined the honeysprites in the treetops. The Protector nearest was not the only one of her escort she did not recognize, in fact, only a couple of faces were familiar. Most of the men were older with broad-shoulders and uncompromising faces. Kest had chosen his most experienced Protectors to keep her safe, she realized, but rather than feeling reassured, she found herself searching the trees.

'Which clan are you from, Protector?' she asked to distract herself.

'Renclan, Leader Kiraon.'

'I've not been there,' she admitted. How was she to lead a people she had never met?

'We have been blessed with good health and few accidents, at least in the seasons of your growing, but your mother visited us often. She had a taste for Renclan song.'

'She sang?'

'She had a very sweet voice and graced us with it many a time.' He smiled. 'Do you sing, Leader Kiraon?'

Kira shook her head. Her father had demanded quiet decorum in the Bough, and her time had been taking up memorizing herbal lists and remedies anyway, not in learning song-words.

'I'm surprised,' he said kindly. 'Your mother has bequeathed you her face and it's said the voice and the countenance often go together.'

Kira ground the sweetchew between her teeth as she waited for the tightness in her throat to ease. 'What are you named, Protector?' she asked, when she was able.

'Lethrin, Leader Kiraon.'

'When things are more settled, Lethrin, I will visit your longhouse and hear the music my mother enjoyed. Do you still play it?'

'Most nights, Leader Kiraon. And you will be a most honored guest.'

They stopped to eat at midday and Kira settled under an ashael to take her meal of nutbread and fruit. She longed to hear the ashael sing in the wind, and she smiled as a breeze woke, and a soft hum sounded in the branches above.

As a child, she had believed all Allogrenia's trees sang to each other or whispered when the day was still. She imagined news of courtings, pledgings, and birthings being passed from leaf-tip to leaf-tip through the entire length and breadth of the forest, but she had never imagined them speaking of death.

Her mother had died and others too, and she had joined her father and brothers in the slow processions through the trees. She had seen the newly turned earth at the Eights too, when her gathering had taken her that way, but she had *heard* nothing. Death had been all around her, but she had been deaf to it, and now death had visited *her*.

Panic threatened, and she visualized the falzon bandage binding a wound until she calmed. The ashael's song was no longer soothing and she packed away her food and scrambled to her feet. The Protectors did the same, and when the Leader clipped out an order, they took up their positions again and moved off.

Kira wished the council was over with and she was on her way back to the Warens. Miken had broken uncounted seasons of tradition by scheduling the council at the new moon, rather than the full one. He had said there were too many important things to be addressed to delay any further, but Kira knew attacks were more likely at the full moon.

The first Clancouncil with a new leader could be held at any longhouse, including Kashclan, but Miken had chosen Sherclan. She had been disappointed it was not at Kashclan, having hoped to see Tenerini, Mikini and the rest of her kin, but Miken wanted to avoid the impression of favoritism. He had warned her against seeking his or Marren of Morclan's advice at the Clancouncil for the same reason.

Marren was seen as his ally, he had told her, and Kira sighed as she considered the pitfalls she needed to avoid, to be a good leader. It was going to be hard, given she had no idea what most of them were! As leader, she should be able to seek advice from whoever she chose, or at least, from those best able to provide it.

Her father had not liked Miken *or* Marren because they had questioned his authority, unlike the other clanleaders, who had simply fallen into line, and her heart sank as she realized the council probably remained divided.

There was so much she did not know! Perhaps if she made a terrible job of the leadership, they would appoint someone else. A feeling of relief swept over her at the prospect, tempered by knowing there was no avoiding this first meeting.

She knew that councils began with formal welcomes and after that, she supposed Kest would outline his plans for the protection of the longhouses, and then any issues Kest or the clanleaders raised would be discussed. Her role would be to ensure that discussions remained orderly, and to call for a dividing when they had run their course. It sounded simple enough when Miken had described it last night, but now even managing such routine matters seemed overwhelming.

What if the councilors ignored her? Tenedren and Ketten would probably be courteous, but not Dakresh, who had opposed her appointment, and she wondered suddenly if Miken had chosen Dakresh's longhouse to appease him.

Marren could be relied on to be polite too, and probably Kemrick, who Miken described as quiet and thoughtful. But Kemrick would likely agree with Berendash on most things, Miken had said, because their octads had an *alliance*. The idea of octads joining against the rest of the Tremen had so shocked her, she had not thought to ask what type of alliance it was.

Then there was Sanden of Renclan, Tenedren of Kenclan, and Ketten of Barclan, who she knew nothing about. In fact, apart from Miken, she could not claim to know much about *any* of the Clanleaders. They had come to the Bough rarely, usually at the Feast of Turning or Thanking, and she had taken no interest in them or in her father and Merek's discussion of them or Clancouncil business.

From what Miken said, the Clanleaders had their own individual wants and needs, and she wondered how her father had managed to maintain any unity at all. It was soon going to be horribly clear that he'd had a whole lot of skills she lacked. She just hoped her brief stint as leader did not turn out to be costly for the Tremen.

Soft purple lines of smoke threaded through the branches and there was an excited whoop as a child scampered off, but the longhouse's guard of Protectors would have already passed on news of their arrival. The smoke thickened, heavy with the scent of fallowood, for fallowoods grew thick about the longhouse, and her escort drew closer, more for ceremonial reasons, she guessed, than protection.

The silvered wood of the Sherclan longhouse emerged from the trees, its shingles covered in shaggyman and mottlecrest, its shutters thrown wide to welcome the summer air. Voices echoed, a mix of children's giggles and the sterner tones of the adults who quietened them, and she saw that Sherclansmen and women had gathered in front of the building, and along the path to its entranceway. A hush fell as they saw her and Kira quelled the urge to flee back into the trees. She swallowed her fear, straightened, and advanced slowly towards them.

10

Her arrival was not the ordeal she had feared. People smiled warmly, and hands were extended in welcome to clasp hers. 'Kashclan thanks Sherclan, Kashclan thanks Sherclan,' she repeated, her voice thick with emotion. A Sherclansman waited at the heavily carved door, too young to be Dakresh, his light brown hair worn to his shoulders in the Sherclan manner.

'Sherclan welcomes Tremen Leader Feailner Kiraon,' he said formally, and bowed low.

He looked familiar, despite Kira knowing she had not met him before. 'Tremen Leader Kiraon thanks Sherclan,' she replied. She wondered if Dakresh's absence were some sort of insult and if so, how she should respond, but the young man's face held only respect. 'I am Clanleader Dakresh's elder son, Sener. Please accept my father's apologies for him not being here to welcome you in person.'

He was the brother of the boy she had met near the Sarnia caves, and their resemblance explained why he looked familiar. She smiled and moved past him into the hall. It had been decorated with garlands of starflower and lissium, the white and pink striking against the darker wood of the walls. A large table stood at the hall's centre with stern-faced men seated around it and their conversation ceased as Kira appeared. Sener courteously led her to her seat at the head of the table and withdrew.

All the chairs were taken except one, obviously Dakresh's, and she wondered again whether he absented himself in protest. Kest was not there either, but he wasn't

87

a clanleader so maybe protocol dictated he join them later. The men rose so she remained standing, staring stolidly ahead, and taking care not to look at Miken or Marren.

There was a clearing of throats and then the council spoke as one. 'The clanleaders welcome Tremen Leader Feailner Kiraon. May her healing be strong, her hand gentle, and her ears open to the thoughts of her people.'

The greeting was clearly part of some traditional welcome that Miken had neglected to tell her about or to describe the expected response. She moistened her lips. 'I thank the clanleaders for their welcome. I will heal with all my heart, gather without harm to the green and growing, and listen to those who would have words with me.'

There was a pause, but Kira kept her gaze fixed on the end of the hall. There was obviously something more expected but mumbling something meaningless was not going to mend the situation. The silence stretched until it became uncomfortable and then the Clanleaders sat down. Kira breathed a sigh of relief and was about to follow suit, when one of the clanleaders rose again. He wore the reddish-brown tunic of Tarclan, but her mind had gone blank.

'Clanleader Kemrick,' he said, with a gentle smile. Kira was so grateful to him she felt like falling on his neck, but she simply nodded. 'As we enjoy Sherclan's hospitality,' he continued softly, 'it is Clanleader Dakresh's privilege to deliver the next part of the welcome but, as he has been delayed, I hope there will be no objection if I deliver it on his behalf.' He glanced around the assembly and there were nods and murmurs of approval.

'Tremen Leader Feailner Kiraon, you have come to the leadership suddenly and in tragic circumstances, but none here doubt your strength or skill to perform its duties. We understand, however, that you may not be familiar with every aspect of the council, and I hope you will take no insult if we,' Kemrick gestured to those present, 'help you in these early meetings. I too am new to the council, so I know how puzzling it can seem.'

'I thank you,' said Kira.

Kemrick's face was full of kindness and she sensed he was not the only clanleader who wanted her to do well. Her plan to renounce the leadership at the end of the meeting was starting to seem churlish.

'The mark of the Tremen Leadership is the ring of rulership,' continued Kemrick solemnly. 'The ring is older than Allogrenia and carries the running horse, mark of our kin in the north, and the alwaysgreen, beloved of we who make our home in its Shelter. In presenting this ring to the leader, the Tremen entrust themselves to the leader's care. In taking it, the leader accepts that trust, *and* the responsibilities that go with it.' He paused. 'Will you take the ring?'

The question took Kira by surprise and she glanced at Miken. He looked nonplussed too. Kemrick had paved the way for her appointment but now he gave her the chance to renounce it. Was the council telling her they only wanted her as leader if she *wanted* to lead them?

The council waited for her answer and she dried her palms on her leggings. 'I've never sought the leadership,' she began hoarsely, and coughed to clear her throat. 'I've been content to gather, to make herbal pastes and potions, to tend the sick and injured. I've never imagined a life beyond that.'

By the 'green, she was making a poor job of this. Feet shuffled, and councilors exchanged glances. 'The gathering of herbs and the making of potions are small things in the affairs of the council,' she began again, 'but Kasheron broke a people for them, and they're the reason the clans labored so hard to establish our gentle, beautiful Allogrenia.'

Her throat tightened but at least she had their attention now and she made herself meet the eyes of each councilor in turn. 'I cannot force my will upon you and nor will I try. I am a Healer, that is all. But I pledge to you that I will never stop striving to heal and that I will never stop struggling to keep healing strong, and that I will fight to the end of my strength to rebuild and reclaim all the Shargh have tried to take from us. If that is not enough, then you must choose another leader.' Her knees shook, and she sat down, her gaze on the table.

'It is enough for me,' said Kemrick gravely. 'Is it enough for my fellow councilors?'

There must have been nods for Kemrick's voice sounded again. 'Bring the ring of rulership.'

Kira forced her head up in time to see a small wooden box being passed from hand to hand around the table before it came to rest in front of her. 'The leader must assume her duties willingly,' prompted Kemrick.

The box was of alwaysgreen, heavily carved, and still smelled spicy, despite its age. Kira slid the lid open and froze, unprepared for the torrent of emotions. The last time she had seen this ring was on her father's hand, the moment before the blow, and now it rested on a bed of brilliant red cloth.

No dye in Allogrenia made such a color and confirmed the box, like the ring, came from the north. The cloth's color was as repellent as the ring, but the council waited, and she braced herself and took the ring out. It was heavy and cold, and she had to resist the urge to hurl it from her.

'The ring can be worn around the neck if it's too large for the hand,' said Kemrick. 'I have read that Leader Feailner Sinaki and Leader Feailner Tesrina wore it so.'

Kira undid the thong Kest had given her with its carved mira kiraon and slipped the ring on. It slid down and came to rest on the bird's wooden wings, and Kira was relieved that the wings kept the chill metal off her skin. Then chairs grated as the councilors stood. 'The clans welcome Leader Feailner Kiraon.'

Kira swallowed dryly. She could scarcely believe she had just passed up the opportunity to escape the leadership. 'I thank the clans for their welcome,' she managed to say, and everyone sat.

Kira had thought the council would spend most of its time discussing the Shargh attacks and strategies for keeping the longhouses and gatherers safe, but they seemed content to speak of more mundane matters. Perhaps they waited for Kest. She was tempted to ask when, or indeed *whether* he was going to join them, but was prevented by the thought that as leader, she should probably already know.

Kest did not appear until the shutters had been pulled closed against the evening dew, the day having passed in the discussion of the trading of black, brown and bitternuts between the octads, the state of the withyweed harvest, and the fish levels in the Drinkwater and Everflow. Kira had said little, for the talk had been surprisingly amiable, and there had been no need for divisions, but she had learned much.

Provisions had arrived at the Bough without any effort by those who lived there. Food had been brought from the octads *and* cloth, which Sendra and the previous helpers had dyed and sewn into shirts, tunics, or trousers, or which Lern had soaked in weatherall for boots. The Bough was the heart of healing; those who dwelt there didn't spend their strength on foraging and making clothes.

Kira had occasionally helped Mikini weave on her visits to the Kashclan longhouse, but it had been fun, like games of hide with Tresen. It was only now she realized the effort involved by those of the longhouses to supply the Bough as well as their own needs.

Kest arrived just as the council broke their discussions to refresh themselves with fruit and thornyflower tea. Kira was speaking with Tenedren, having continued to avoid Miken and Marren, and happened to face the door when it opened. Despite his clean clothing and gleaming hair, Kest looked grim, and almost as tired as the last time she had seen him.

His expression flicked to neutral as the clanleaders turned and he smiled as he exchanged greetings and moved through the assembly to her side. 'Congratulations, Tremen Leader Feailner Kiraon,' he said with a small bow.

'Thank you, Commander Kest,' she said, and ensured her voice carried to the rest of the gathering. 'I congratulate you also on your promotion and ask that you simply call me Tremen Leader Kiraon like the council. After all, the Tremen know I am a woman, I hope.'

There was a polite titter but the lines round Kest's mouth deepened, and Kira bit her lip. The remark had sounded like a game of point-scoring and she briefly touched his arm. 'Come Commander. I will get you some tea, and then we must resume the council.' They moved away to the cooking place where the pot had been set back on the coals and Kira filled a cup and handed it to him. 'There's fish and nutbread too,' she said. 'You should eat.' Kest shook his head and Kira watched him sip his tea. 'Tell me what's happened, Commander.'

'What makes you think something's happened?'

'Your face when you arrived.'

'It seems I'll have to be more careful when I'm around you, Tremen Leader Kiraon.'

'I would rather you were honest.'

'I've always been that with you,' he said, his intense blue eyes boring into hers.

Kira's face warmed. 'I know. You've often told me how stubborn and irresponsible I am.' Kest's face remained set and Kira sobered. 'Please tell me what's wrong.'

'Dakresh's son is missing.'

'Sener? But he was here before.'

Kest moved impatiently. 'Not him. His younger son, Bern.'

Kira's breath caught. It had Bern she had seen near the Sarnia caves, pledging to return to his longhouse in just a few days, *carrying a pack that could sustain him for many*.

'Dakresh thought he was visiting friends at Kenclan,' Kest was saying, 'but he never arrived. Either there's been an accident or else . . .'

'You've been searching for him?' she asked, feeling sick to the stomach.

Kest rubbed his face wearily. 'I've mainly been fighting Dakresh. The old fool's all for storming off to the Sentinels on his own. It's understandable, I suppose. Sener and Bern are all he has left from three bondings. His first bondmate and Sener's mother died of fever, and Bern's mother died in childbirth.'

'Where's Dakresh now?' Kira forced herself to ask.

'He's agreed to stay at the Kenclan longhouse in return for me sending a patrol beyond the Kenclan Second Eight.' Kira stared at the empty seat at the table. She should have insisted Bern go home; she should have told Kest she'd seen him. Kest's warm hand closed over hers. 'It might yet turn out well, Kira. Bern's thirteen seasons. Boys of that age—'

'I saw him.'

'What?'

'When I was searching for the fireweed. I saw him.'

'Stinking heart-rot! Why in the 'green didn't you tell me?'

'I don't know. I . . . he said he was going to the Sarnia caves. He said he'd been there before. He was excited about the caves, about seeing new things in the octad . . .' Kira trailed off under Kest's furious gaze.

'I *told* you how dangerous it was! Do my words mean *nothing* to you?'

'He pledged me to return home in a few days. I didn't see the harm . . .' said Kira miserably.

Kest's cup slammed down on the table and Kira was aware of the clanleaders' sudden silence. Kest was too, for his voice dropped to a hiss. 'He's probably dead!'

There was a polite cough and Kira turned to see Miken at her elbow, his gaze darting between them. 'The council's ready to resume,' he said.

11

Kira made her way numbly back to her seat. How could she have possibly accepted the leadership? She must have been mad! She had no sense of responsibility, no ability to think ahead, to see the consequences of her actions; to plan, to lead! She closed her eyes in dread. Bern! Surely he hadn't been taken? He was only thirteen, the same age as . . .

Kest was speaking and she dragged her eyes open, thankful the councilors were focused on him, all except for Miken, whose questioning gaze was fixed firmly on her. She unclenched her hands from the table's edge and struggled to compose herself.

'. . . made up of members of each clan,' Kest was saying. 'And so, the Renclan longhouse will be guarded by Protectors drawn from Renclansmen, and the Sherclan longhouse by Protectors drawn from Sherclan, and so on. This will increase the speed of foraging expeditions because clans know their own octads best. And the quicker they can forage, the less risk there will be of attack. *When* foraging occurs must also be considered. Both attacks have been at the full moon and it makes sense that outsiders would choose the time of greatest moonlight.

'I suggest each longhouse cease foraging at the waxing half-moon and resumes after the waning half-moon. Clanleaders might have to consider extra storage at their respective longhouses to accommodate the change. Protectors will patrol the lands circled by the Second Eight. These patrols will be men drawn from all the clans and will be concentrated in the north-east octads of Kenclan and Barclan, closest to the Shargh's lands.'

'What of healing?' asked Kemrick. 'Is that to continue in the Warens?'

'Yes. The Warens are easiest to guard and it will take time to rebuild the Bough, *if* it is to be rebuilt.'

There was a stunned silence and Kemrick was the first to recover. 'But surely Commander, the Bough *must* be rebuilt.'

'That, of course, is for the council to decide,' said Kest. 'But remember, councilors, that we don't know how long the Shargh attacks will last, or indeed, why they started. The Shargh have occupied lands to the north-east since Kasheron's time, but we have no record of attacks until now. Why have they begun? We don't know. What is their purpose? We don't know that either.

'To burn the Bough, they passed Kenclan and Barclan longhouses, both unguarded. If their intention was simply to kill, it would have been easy to start there, but if their intention was to kill *healing*, to kill our *leadership*, then they've all but succeeded. But again, we don't know why they would want to do so.'

Kira sucked in air as Kest tore away the fragile images of falzon bandages she used to keep the horror at bay. *If their intention had been to kill healing, to kill our leadership, then they've all but succeeded.* Kemrick quietly passed her a cup of water and Kira clutched it with both hands, her eyes fixed sightlessly on the cup's patterning.

'If healing must be hidden away, they have won anyway,' said Miken.

'They won't have *won* while healing survives,' retorted Sanden. 'Everything Commander Kest says makes sense. What's the point of spending our strength rebuilding the

Bough, if the cost of protecting it leaves the longhouses vulnerable? We've already lost many men and if the attacks continue season after season, and we lose more each time, there will soon be too few to protect the longhouses, and they too will fall. It will be the end of Allogrenia.'

Kira's head filled with the Bough as she had last seen it and she drove her nails into the table in an attempt to use this new pain to mask the old. No one noticed. Miken's voice had risen as he gesticulated at Sanden; Kemrick and Berendash leaned across the table to exchange words with Marren; and Ketten and Tenedren pushed their chairs from the table as they shared a private conversation.

Only Kest was silent, his gaze on her. No doubt her turmoil added to his poor opinion. If only this meeting were done with and she was away from here, the leaf-litter under her feet, the cry of the mira kiraon in her ears. But there would be none of that if Kest had his way. She would spend her time in the Warens, eating and sleeping in its sunless gloom until the Shargh got bored with their killing and went away. And if they never got bored?

Why had they come? To kill healing? Or to kill the leadership? It was the same thing anyway. And Sanden was right. If they continued to lose men, Allogrenia would be no more. Feseren and Sanaken dead in the first attack; twenty-three in the Bough's fires; five more before the fireweed had burned away the rot. Twenty men still lay in the Warens, some who would take another season to recover, some who would never recover.

With less than a thousand Tremen spread between the eight clans, it would not be long before Allogrenia was indefensible. Kest had a plan but it was not a solution, just an eking out of an existence in an ever-tightening circle around each longhouse, while healing remained buried in the Warens.

Nausea surged, and she struggled to her feet, desperate to halt the tide of bleakness before it overwhelmed her. 'Councilors!' Her voice was drowned by the hubbub. 'Councilors!' she bawled, surprising even herself as every face turned to her. 'Kindly resume your seats so I can hear from you in a more orderly fashion.' By the 'green! She sounded like her father.

She waited for the last chair to grate back into place. 'I've heard Commander Kest's suggestions on how we should proceed, now I would like to hear yours. Clanleader Sanden, have you anything to add to your earlier comments?' Sanden shook his head and she turned to Kemrick. 'Then perhaps Clanleader Kemrick can share his thoughts, followed by the leaders to his right, until all present have spoken.'

Kira resumed her seat and the attention of the gathering swung to Kemrick. Most of the clanleaders agreed with Kest's plans, although some took a long time to say so and Kira had to suppress more than one sigh. Kemrick, Miken, and Marren seemed to be the only ones who had thought beyond the here and now, and Kemrick expressed their views the most eloquently. To live behind a ring of swords would be to live like those in the north, he said. If that was to be the price of their survival, were they prepared to pay it? Many of the leaders were dismissive of such a pessimistic picture, but it resonated deeply within Kira.

'I thank you all for your contributions,' she said, after the last speaker Ketten had fallen silent. 'And for your patience in allowing each other to speak.' So far, so good.

'And I thank Commander Kest for giving us so much to think about.' What next? The Shargh terrified her, but she wasn't prepared to spend the rest of her life living underground.

'I think Commander Kest's plan is a good one, *for the present*. I will remain in the Warens until the last of the wounded are well enough to return to their longhouses to complete their recovery there. I expect this to be in three to four moons unless we receive more wounded. During this time, I will finish recording my Healer knowing, *with* the help of the other Healers. There will be several sheafs made and stowed in different locations. There must never again be a time when all that Kasheron bequeathed us is held by a single person.'

There were nods and murmurings of agreement. 'But,' she continued, 'I think Commander Kest's plan that Protectors guard their own longhouses is a poor one, and I ask him to reconsider it.'

Kest's sympathetic expression vanished. 'On what basis?' he demanded. 'Do you disagree foraging would be more effective when aided by Protectors familiar with their own octad?'

'No.'

Kest's eyebrows rose in exasperation. 'Then what?'

'Because of what the forests offer, the longhouses are almost a half day's walk from each other,' said Kira.

'You tell us nothing new, Leader Kiraon,' said Ketten.

'You're saying we are already isolated from one another?' prompted Kemrick.

Kira nodded. 'Assigning Protectors to their own octads will increase this isolation. We will no longer be Tremen but Barclansmen and Barclanswomen, or Renclansmen and Renclanswomen.'

'That hasn't happened so far,' pointed out Kest, 'and I see no reason why it should happen in the future. The longhouses have always been separated by a long walk.'

'Yes, but there's always been mixing,' said Kira. 'Protector training brings the young men of all clans together, and seeds friendships and visitations that continue long after their training has finished. They meet their friends' sisters, and acquaintances are renewed each Feast of Turning and Thanking, celebrations that will cease because the Warens are too small to accommodate them.'

'I can't agree with you Tremen Leader Kiraon,' said Kest. 'There will still be opportunities for people to forage in each other's octads as they've always done, under protection of course.'

'If the Shargh attacks continue, people might be reluctant to risk it,' pointed out Miken.

'Surely this is a small thing,' interrupted Ketten, 'if it keeps us safe.'

Kira drew a steadying breath. 'Earlier Clanleader Kemrick raised the question of what it means to be Tremen. I think it's an important question. What are we prepared to do to survive? What are we prepared to change? To trade off? To give up?'

There was a scrape of chairs as people moved restlessly. The councilors were weary of the topic, realized Kira, and wanted to vote to end the council and start the journey back to their longhouses. The sun was sinking and at the hall's far end, a young Sherclanswoman quietly lit the lamps.

Ketten glanced at the lamplighter too. 'It must be time for the division,' he said.

'It doesn't need to be one thing or the other,' said Kemrick suddenly.

100

Ketten peered at him irritably. 'What mean you?'

'As long as there are Protectors from the clan's own octad guarding, *and* from other octads, both Commander Kest's and Tremen Leader Kiraon's concerns would be met. Would they not?' He looked at Kest and Kira in turn. They nodded.

'Praise the 'green,' muttered Ketten.

'Are we agreed then, that for the next few moons, Protectors will be deployed as outlined by Commander Kest, but with mixed groups assigned to each longhouse, while I will ensure our healing knowing is recorded once more?' asked Kira. There was a chorus of assent. 'Then there is no need of a division?' she asked, her eyes on Ketten.

'No division leader, please, no division,' said Ketten with a broad smile.

12

The world of the Warens was like a fractured version of the world above, rearranged in the wrong order. Day blended with night into an even grey; heat and cold became a tepid dankness; sounds from nearby caverns were muffled and those from far away amplified. Kira's senses felt dulled by the Warens' endless tedium and her body afflicted by a low level of weariness.

She yawned, set down her pen and stretched, but the scratch of Tresen's pen continued. He looked like a hanawey hovering over its prey: clean sheets of patchet paper scattered to one side, neat stacks of Writings to the other.

What must be recorded seemed endless: findings and gatherings; preparations and treatments; the signs and symptoms of fevers and chills, breaks and sprains; the stitching of cuts; the salving of burns; the complications of childbirth and old age; the consequences of knocks to the head; falls . . . the lists went on and on, written in Tremen and Onespeak.

She had started with fireweed: the place and manner of its growth, its gathering, preparation, and ministering. *Fire with flatswords brings the bane, fire without brings life again.* Fire was the fever brought on by whatever the Shargh put on their flatswords, and fire *without* was the fevered heat that came *without* flatswords but with fireweed, that burned the flatswords' rot away. Never again would the meaning of the rhyme be lost, even if the Shargh killed every Healer in the Warens. But fireweed was just one herb of thousands.

She rubbed her neck. Pledging to record her knowing while sitting in a longhouse filled with sunlight and birdsong was one thing; doing it day after day or was it night after night, was another. The problem was she knew too much!

Since the age of four, she had been trailing around the Herbery, looking, and listening. By seven, she had gathered beyond the First Eight. She could not remember when she had first read the Herbal Sheaf or felt broken bones come together under her fingers. The knowing seemed to have always been there, and now it must be recorded.

It was no use grumbling. She owed her understanding to the Healers who had gone before, and now she must preserve it for those who followed, no matter how wearisome the task. She gulped down a cup of tepid water, grimaced and wiped her mouth. Why did the Warens' water taste so different to the Drinkwater? It was as if it had distilled the walls' mustiness.

Tresen's hand moved from ink pot to paper, ink pot to paper, with mesmerizing regularity, and Kira sighed. At least they only had to do one copy, Arlen and Paterek busy in one of the storage rooms transcribing their work multiple times. Recording her knowing would soon be faster too, for she would have more time.

Several of the wounded had already returned to their longhouses under escort, and over the next few days, others would follow. By late summer, the Haelen should be empty, *if* there were no more attacks, and then she would be free to leave the Warens, *if* Kest allowed it. Her fingers drummed the table.

'I've almost finished the gathering sites for sorren and annin,' said Tresen. 'Do you want me to start on the mints next?'

'Yes,' said Kira vaguely, her thoughts still on Kest. 'Icemint, bluemint, silvermint, and can you include silversalve? It's similar in habit and use.' Tresen nodded and his hand resumed its journeying. Kira wondered if Kest were back. It must be five nights since the council, no, probably six. If Kest *were* back in the Warens, he had not deigned to visit, which meant Bern was probably safely ensconced in his own longhouse enduring no more than Dakresh's wrath.

She rolled a stub of patchet paper idly along the table and gazed at the bundles of sorren, serewort and winterbloom stacked along the wall beside her mattress. It was pointless pretending all was well. If Kest *were* back, he would have come to see Kesilini, and probably taken the opportunity to give her another tongue-lashing over Bern.

She crushed the paper under her fingers. Kest's absence could only mean Bern had not been found, *or* that Kest had come under attack. Why in the 'green had she not insisted Bern go back immediately, *or* told Kest she had seen him?

Kenclan ran north-east and the moon must be nearly full again. It was a dangerous time to be abroad, even for a patrol. She used to climb high into the alwaysgreens at the full moon, to gaze out over a canopy as silver as the seas of the older tales. Instead of mighty sea birds rising and falling above its waves, hanaweys and frostkings had owned the skies, but now that pleasure had been stolen from her too.

A groan sounded, and she rose and went to the hanging, but Arlen was already there, and water tinkled as he moistened a cloth and pressed it to the wounded man's face. The man's restless movements stilled, and she turned back to the Writings and stood considering where the copies should be stowed. In one of the longhouses perhaps, and here, and in the more obscure caverns? The Sarnia Room was too obvious. If the Shargh found their way into the Warens, they would destroy everything in it.

She yawned again and rubbed her eyes. She did not know if she were tired or just sick of sitting. The lamp oil was low and the cover full of silver moths pit-pitting against it. One had fallen in and moved feebly on its surface. She lifted the cover and hooked it out with her finger, but its wings were broken, and it lay where she left it.

Silver moths would be thick in the trees outside too, drawn by the moon. What she would not give to dash along the Drinkwater Path, to feel the dawn air bright against her face, to smell the wet leaf-fall and leaves and berries.

Tresen's pen had fallen silent and she looked at him as he yawned. 'Why don't you go to bed?' she said. 'You've done enough for one day.' His skin was sallow in the lamplight and his eyes hollow. He had lost weight *and* his smile since he had been confined in the Warens. He had always been quick to tease, to joke, to laugh, but not anymore. 'You should go back to your longhouse for a while. Tenerini hasn't seen you since this began, or Mikini. They must miss you, and you them. And what of Seri?'

'Seri's safe in her own longhouse, which is the best place for her, and it's not fair to leave you to do all this on your own.'

'Arlen and Paterek can help,' said Kira.

'They don't know enough Onespeak.' Tresen stoppered the ink pot and wiped his hands. 'Besides, I'm not going back until you can come with me. It's your longhouse too remember. Tenerini's always wanted another daughter.'

He reached over and took her hand. 'And I've always wanted another sister.'

'Your mother's been kind to me,' she said softly, 'and if I weren't leader I'd come. But I *am* leader and that changes everything.'

Tresen's hand tightened on hers. 'No leader has to do *everything* on their own, Kira. You could—'

A rhythmic thump sounded, faint at first but growing louder. The unmistakable march of feet and they froze as the tramp seemed to pause outside the training room, then passed on. Kira's breath hissed and Tresen half rose from his seat then slumped back. 'No more wounded, at least not yet,' he said. 'But the moon waxes and Kest's still beyond the Third Eight.'

Kira's head jerked around. 'The Third Eight! How know you this?'

Tresen began gathering the unused patchet paper into a pile. 'Penedrin told me. You knew Dakresh's son was still missing?'

'Yes.'

'Apparently, he was sighted near the Sarnia caves, so Kest's gone looking. Personally, I doubt there's much hope of finding him. The octad is so big it would take a moon to search it properly.' He cleaned the pen, lay it ready, and put on his jacket. 'Bern knew the dangers. He should have kept to his longhouse. His foolishness risks the lives of others now.'

'He's only thirteen!'

'Old enough to know better.' Tresen's dark brown eyes came to hers. 'There's twenty-one men in a patrol, Kira. That's twenty-one men who might be wounded or killed; twenty-one men who won't be there to protect their longhouses.'

'Are you saying they *shouldn't* look for him?' she demanded.

'We lost the equivalent of a patrol, either dead or wounded, in the attack on the Bough. If that happens every full moon, how long do you think we can last? Do the sums, Kira, I have.'

'Every life is important, Tresen!'

'Do you think I don't know that? I'm Kashclan, Kira, like you! Do you think—' He cut off whatever he was about to say and forced a smile. 'I don't want to argue with you, clanmate. I'm going to take your advice and get some sleep. I suggest you do the same.' He leaned over and kissed her on the cheek. 'I wish you a good night.'

The curtain fell back into place but Tresen's words echoed in her head. It was more or less what Sanden had said at the council, but Tresen had gone even further. Tresen had suggested the Tremen might have to decide whose life was worth more; that they might have to trade one life for another, in this case, Bern's life for the lives of the patrol.

She licked her dry lips. If Tresen were right, next time it might not be the life of a wayward boy to be sacrificed, but that of a laboring woman, whose welfare might be deemed less worthy than the leader's, and the leader's patrol of Protectors.

She poured herself a cup of water and gulped it down. Surely it wouldn't come to that? Surely this time would pass? And everything would go back to the way it was? Summer mornings in the scent-rich Herbery? The sweet notes of Kandor's pipe drifting through the hall? The hope mocked her, and brought with it the unbearable, inescapable pain of Kandor's death.

She collapsed onto her mattress, curled up, and head cradled in her arms. Sleep brought no rest, just dreams of Kandor, his hair haloed with lamplight as she had dragged her hands from his and condemned him to death.

She groaned, and her thoughts went to the pouch of everest in her pack, as they so often did. Half a leaf would bring a sleep of many days and a whole leaf send her to where Kandor now dwelt, in a place empty of memory and pain.

How she longed to go there. But she had not the right. She was the leader now, the holder of all healing, the person able to stop the deaths of other Kandors. She pulled herself to her knees and then to her feet and stumbled back to the table. Tremen and Onespeak, she thought numbly, and started to write.

A frostking called amongst the branches above him but Kest did not raise his head. He sat slumped against an espin trunk gazing into space. He was filthy, his shirt stiff with dried sweat, his hands blackened by soil. Half his patrol was secreted among the trees, the other half wrapped carelessly in their sleeping-sheets. They had not set a proper camp, just crawled into their sheets without bothering to eat. He had not eaten either, the stench of putrefying flesh too strong to stomach food.

Bern had been dead for many days, although even a couple in the summer heat would have been enough. But heat alone had not caused his sickening disfigurement. Bern had not died from a single stab wound but from many. His death had been agonizing. Kest unclipped his waterskin and took a long, slow swig.

The simplest explanation was the Shargh were barbarous, had chanced upon a lone boy, and enjoyed some sport. But that left too many questions unanswered: the line of slashed trees to the Third Eight where they had found Bern's pack; the single boot they had discovered as they had followed the trampled growth north-east; and Bern's body dumped like refuse near the Sentinels. Why had not the Shargh killed him where they had captured him?

Kest stowed his waterskin, hauled himself upright and picked his way between his men to the deeper darkness of the alwaysgreen. Someone kept vigil: Nandrin, Bern's clanmate. He rose as Kest approached but Kest waved him back and settled beside him.

The darkness hid the new-turned earth, but the air told of where they had cut the turfs with their swords and dug out a resting place between the roots with hands and sticks. Patrols did not carry shovels and he wondered whether it was just one of the changes he would have to make.

Nandrin sat with his head down, and his hands hanging slackly between his knees, and Kest glanced at him and then back at the moon-stippled shapes of the men who rested behind him.

'I hope Clanleader Dakresh forgives us for not bringing Bern home,' he said softly.

Nandrin looked up, his face like a skull in the moonlight. 'At least he is safe now,' he said thickly. 'The alwaysgreen Shelters him.'

'But too distant for Dakresh to visit. I don't think his old bones will carry him this far.'

'Nor his heart.' Nandrin's eyes were dark pools. 'Who would do this? Who would do such a thing to a boy?'

'People who love death, not life.'

'Outsiders,' spat Nandrin. 'Northerners! Murderers!'

The Shargh were not Northerners, but Kest let it go, glad that Nandrin at least was talking, unlike Kira, who had never spoken of her grief. He wondered why he thought of her now, when so much else crowded his head.

Nandrin wiped his sleeve across his face. '*The roots have taken him,*' he said hoarsely.

Kest gripped his arm. '*The tree grown strong from him, the new leaves spun from him.*'

'*The wind sung songs of him . . .*' Nandrin choked to a stop.

'*His story told,*' finished Kest quietly.

As if in answer, a breeze riffled the canopy, and as the alwaysgreen leaves whispered, Kest stood. 'We leave at dawn, Nandrin. Time to rest.'

Nandrin rose too and Kest watched Nandrin crawl into his sleeping-sheet. Moonlight lay in bright medallions over the leaf-litter and his jaw tightened, as he surveyed the close-growing espins. A waxing moon and heavy cover. It suited the Shargh well. He turned back to camp, settled under the tree, and sharpened his sword.

13

In the highest sorcha on the slope, Palansa sat on the hide of rulership and surveyed the assembled warriors. Her fingers locked, bone against bone, her palms greasy with sweat as the warriors' eyes flicked over her. Arkendrin had positioned himself directly in front, with Irdodun and Urpalin at either side. Now and again he murmured to Irdodun, and the lesser man smirked, but Arkendrin's eyes never left her.

Palansa shifted her attention to Irdodun. The man was like the stink-beetles that burrowed in the ebis droppings. They might make grand and intricate tunnels, but they would never be more than stink-beetles in dung. She smiled contemptuously, and her confidence surged as Irdodun dropped his eyes. She felt as if she had struck the first blow. Tarkenda nodded discreetly to her side, and Palansa cleared her throat, and waited till the rumble of conversation ceased.

'This Speak I call on behalf of my unborn son, who, when he greets the day, will be the first-born son of Erboran himself, the first-born son of Ergardrin, continuing the line of rulership the Sky Chiefs bequeathed us. I call this Speak because a matter of great importance has arisen, a matter which affects us all.' Palansa moved her gaze from one warrior to another as she spoke, passing over her allies, Ormadon and Irsulalin and their kin, in the same unhurried way as she passed over Arkendrin and Irdodun.

'The Sky Chiefs honor us with life and they take us home at its ending, so that we might dwell forever in their realm. In return, we honor them.' She paused and brought her attention back to Irdodun. 'Yet some amongst you dishonor the Sky Chiefs by hunting and spilling blood during the time the Sky Chiefs decree no blood should be spilt. Irdodun, I call upon you to explain your dishonor.'

'I have no Voice, Chief-wife.'

'I grant you one for this occasion,' said Palansa.

'You cannot do that, Chief-wife, without dishonoring those you claim to honor,' said Arkendrin. 'I must speak on Irdodun's behalf, for it is I who led the hunt, as you might know.'

Tarkenda had warned Palansa Irdodun couldn't speak, but Palansa had been desperate to avoid confronting Arkendrin. She managed to keep her face impassive, but her heart thundered as Arkendrin raised his hands theatrically.

'We teeter on the brink of our very destruction,' he boomed. 'Do we plunge to our doom, or do we seize what is rightfully ours? Look around you. The lands thirst; the pastures die. The ebi die too and their mothers eat the stone-trees to keep flesh on their bones. The Grenwah and Shunawah sink and the Thanawah blooms red. Soon sickness will stalk the Grounds and all the while, the highest sorcha lies empty of chief. The best we can hope for is that one day it might house a squalling babe.'

He got to his feet, breaking convention. 'What use is a suckling while in the murk of the south-western treelands, the gold-eyed creature of the Last Telling plots our destruction? Is it dishonor to hunt it? Is it dishonor to seek the destruction of a creature that will destroy us? I am a Shargh warrior! Ordorin's blood runs in my veins! I too am the seed of the warrior the Last Teller chose *above all others* to preserve the Sky Chiefs' warning!

'Should I sit idly in my sorcha while the gold-eyed creature prospers? Should I turn my back on my people?

The Sky Chiefs demand honor, yes, but they gave us spears and swords and tesat to rot the wounds of our enemies. And they gave us warning though the Last Teller, *and* the strength to avert doom it foretold. *If* I have dishonored the Sky Chiefs then, when the time comes, I will beg *their* pardon, but there are none *here* whose pardon I must beg.'

There was a brief silence followed by a wave of muttering. Palansa's mind raced. The insult was deliberate; the challenge to her authority obvious. She could not demand the warriors present defend an unborn child; an unborn child was women's business and not real to them until it was born.

But Arkendrin was real, his chest puffed, his eyes shining as he painted pictures of glory that stirred their blood. Palansa glanced down at Erboran's sword and spears, lying on the hide of rulership before her, and wondered why the Sky Chiefs had left her to fight this battle.

Tarkenda's voice cut through the mutters. 'Sit, Arkendrin. You insult all present by standing.'

It was a mother's rebuke, delivered to a wayward son, not an order delivered with the authority of a chief, and with a mocking smile, Arkendrin slowly sat. The exchanges died away and attention drifted back to Palansa.

'The Sky Chiefs have *never* left us without a chief,' said Palansa quietly. She could not out-bluster Arkendrin and wouldn't try. 'And always it has been the *first-born* son of a *first-born* son. Even when we roamed far beyond the Braghan Mountains, no second-born son has *ever* ruled the Shargh.'

Arkendrin's sneer had a set quality now but Palansa felt no satisfaction. She must win more than a game of words to protect her child. 'In this the Sky Chiefs have held true, and we have honored them for it. Indeed, it has been our willingness to grant them their due that has allowed Arkendrin to boast that he need honor no one here.

'He was but a babe when *his* father was called home and there were those who argued then, as Arkendrin does now, that Ordorin's bloodline should be broken and the Shargh look elsewhere for a chief. But the Sky Chiefs' wishes were respected, and in the season of their choosing, Erboran took the Circlet of Chiefship and ruled wisely and well, as the Sky Chiefs themselves intended.'

Palansa paused. The warriors were quiet, but she sensed they remained unconvinced. Her words had soothed the passions Arkendrin had roused, but not removed their cause. What Arkendrin said was true: the ebi *did* die and the Thanawah *did* run red. Urpalin muttered to the warrior next to him, and there were whispers at the back of the sorcha.

'I thank Arkendrin for using his Voice to remind us of our present troubles,' she said hurriedly, then stopped, as if to lend weight to her next utterance. In truth, her mind had gone blank. Panic threatened, and then the babe pummeled her ribs as if to remind her of what she fought for, and she flattened her palms against her belly to reassure him.

'Life is hard now, I do not pretend it is other, but the Sky Chiefs have granted us many gifts, one of which is strength. Our warriors are mighty hunters, able to run longer than the sun's course across the sky, and to track wolves when only marwings see their spoor. Yet strength is a gift that must be tested, for without adversity, it withers and becomes weakness.' She steadied, knowing what she must say now.

'In withholding the rain, the Sky Chiefs test our strength. Are we to fail their test? Are we to dishonor them and hunt what should not be hunted until the moons of Chief Erboran's mourning have passed? Are we not faithful enough to wait? Not *strong* enough?'

There was absolute silence, then one of the younger warriors spoke. 'I am willing to wait, Chief-wife. I, who have every reason to want the creature dead, will honor the Sky Chiefs.'

The speaker was Urgasen, Urgundin's son, and he sat not with Ursulalin and Ormadon, or with Arkendrin and his cronies, but between. After Urgundin's death, Urgasen had taken his father's place high on the spur, but he was young and his Voice untried. Palansa held her breath as there was a soft ripple of approval, and then exhaled as louder calls of agreement followed.

Palansa avoided looking at Arkendrin, not wanting to appear to gloat. The Shargh were with her for the present and that meant she had won more precious *growing* time for her son. And even when Arkendrin hunted again, there was no guarantee he would find the Healer quickly. Warriors moved restlessly, and some had even started to rise, and she hurriedly spoke the words of ending and watched them file out.

She remained seated even after they had gone, reveling in knowing the Speak was over with. It was Tarkenda who finally struggled to her feet and helped her rise. 'We are a fine pair,' she grunted. 'One woman gnarled with old-man's ache and the other carrying the woman's burden.'

'Not a burden,' said Palansa, as she smoothed down her skirt, 'but a—' The flap flipped open and Ormadon appeared. 'blessing,' she finished. She rolled up the hide of rulership and Ormadon helped her stow it under the bed, then he collected Erboran's spears and leaned them against the wall next to Erboran's sword.

'You spoke well, Chief-wife,' said Ormadon.

'He hates me for it,' said Palansa, taking the circlet from her head and rubbing her sweaty brow.

'His hatred is not new.' Palansa sat next to Tarkenda, and Ormadon settled opposite, and took the bowl of water Tarkenda poured for him. 'You have made the warriors think of the Sky Chiefs, rather than him,' he said. 'That is good. It is dangerous to make the warriors choose between you and Arkendrin; better to make them choose between honoring and not honoring the Sky Chiefs.'

'I thought Arkendrin would win the Speak and continue to hunt the Healer of the Telling,' admitted Tarkenda, 'and that it might have suited our purposes. It would have kept him away from the Grounds, and away from *us*. I hadn't thought to use the argument you did.'

'The result is the same,' said Palansa, as she sipped her water. 'It gives us more time.'

'Not as much as you think,' said Ormadon. 'Arkendrin knows more about the creature now. He knows it is named *owl*, or *kiraon* in the treeman's speech, and he knows it has been weakened by its blood-ties' deaths. He knows there are holes under the trees too, and that it hides in them.'

Palansa paled. 'Irason,' she breathed. 'They must have captured a treeman and Irason read his tongue.'

Ormadon nodded. 'Irdodun puts it about that the hunt is simple now, and that soon the creature's body will be laid out on the spur for all to see. Then Arkendrin will take his rightful place as chief.'

'He will be free to do exactly as he wants then,' said Palansa bitterly. The child quivered inside her, and her gaze went to Erboran's flatsword. The babe prevented her running, even if there were somewhere to run to.

'He is filling the warriors' heads with grand schemes of joining with the Weshargh and Soushargh again and taking back all the lands north of the mountains,' continued Ormadon. 'He wants to be chief of *all* the tracts the Shargh once roamed.'

'He would lead us into a river of blood,' said Tarkenda darkly. 'Does he imagine those lands are ours for the taking? That the Northerners will simply hand them over? The fighting would be worse than in the older days.' Palansa's startled eyes went to hers but Tarkenda kept her attention on Ormadon.

'Arkendrin's tongue has always outpaced his legs,' said Ormadon, as he rose. 'I have heard Urpalin was too ready with the knife, and that he killed the treeman before Arkendrin discovered where the holes were.'

'If that is true, it could take them many moons to find where she hides,' said Palansa hopefully.

Ormadon shrugged. 'It's hard to tell mawkbird from marwing when Arkendrin's followers speak, but knowing Urpalin, the blunder is likely. Whatever the truth, Arkendrin's caught here until the next moon.' He moved to the door. 'Don't be alone Chief-wife,' he said, and ducked through the flap.

'Will your vision come true?' demanded Palansa, as soon as the flap had stilled. 'Is my son to be killed and Arkendrin to take us north?'

'I have told you before that it's unclear to me.'

'Unclear, unclear!' muttered Palansa, pacing up and down the sorcha. 'What's the point of having a vision which can't be read?'

'Ask the Sky Chiefs,' said Tarkenda dryly.

Palansa said nothing and Tarkenda sighed. 'You have done well today, Palansa. Better than I dared hope.'

Palansa turned to her, eyes dark as night. 'Will it be enough?'

Tarkenda's face was grim. 'That too is with the Sky Chiefs.'

14

Kest rinsed the stubble from his face into the bowl and pushed the stub of clear-root back into his pack. He was clean now and, thanks to the clear-root, free of the itching half-beard. He had slept in a bed last night too, even if it were not his own, and despite the awful trip to Dakresh's longhouse, he felt rested for the first time in many days.

Miken had been right to insist he stay the night rather than go straight to the Warens, and right to point out that Kest falling ill from exhaustion would aid no one in Allogrenia. Kest grimaced. He must remember to use that argument on Kira. He made his way down the passageway to the hall, scanning the trees through the open windows as he went. He saw nothing amiss but he wondered what the patrols would report of happenings elsewhere.

The hall was surprisingly crowded considering how early it was. Children giggled as they rolled sour-ripe along the tables to each other, and adults sat with heads close in conversation. This was what he had missed most in the Warens. Not just the fragrant air and tinkle of chimes, but the sounds of normalcy; of happiness.

Miken beckoned him from further down the hall and as he moved through the tables, Kashclansmen and women swiveled, and a group of Protectors hurriedly rose. He waved them back and nodded to the Kashclan he passed.

Miken had poured him a cup of thornyflower and was busy lathing riddleberry spread onto bread. 'I have been thinking on what we spoke of last night,' began Miken softly, without preamble, as he passed Kest the bread. 'I think you're right. The Shargh probably tortured Bern until he told them everything he knew of Kira. The question is, how much did he know?'

Kest took several gulps of his tea. He was still parched from the long march back. 'Kira told me only that she had seen him,' he said, and he'd been too angry to question her further. That had been a mistake.

'She told you at the Clancouncil?' asked Miken. Kest nodded, recalling in irritation that Miken had interrupted them. 'Kira's dear to me,' said Miken, noting his expression, 'not just because she's Kashclan, but because she spent much of her growing here.' His gaze went to Tenerini who took her breakfast with some of the other women. 'We would have taken her as our daughter if Maxen had allowed it,' he said hoarsely. His hand paused on the pot as he cleared his throat, then he refilled Kest's cup. 'We would still take her.'

Kest finished the bread and licked the riddleberries from his fingers. 'If we're right about them hunting her, she would draw the Shargh to you,' said Kest. 'It would risk your entire longhouse.'

'I know. It's best she stays where she is for the time being. But even the Warens might not be safe, especially at the full moon.' He paused. 'Will you tell Kira about Bern?'

'As leader, she has a right to know.'

Miken set his cup down. 'Will you tell her what we suspect about the *nature* of his death?'

'I don't know.' The answer was honest but Kest felt his face warm.

'As Commander of the Protectors, it is of course, your decision, but forgive me if I now speak as someone who knows Kira well. She is stubborn, as you have probably discovered, and single-minded in her passion for healing, necessary qualities in a leader and, no doubt, why the clanleaders agreed to appoint her. But what is less obvious, is her lack of self-interest.'

'Surely that's a good quality in a leader, unlike her recklessness—' Kest faltered as he remembered the clan-link, but Miken nodded, taking no insult.

'Perhaps what I should have said is Kira lacks a sense of self-preservation. She puts others first.'

'I would have thought that was a good quality in a leader too.'

'It is up to a point,' agreed Miken. 'But beyond that, it can be destructive. If Kira believes she's the reason for the Shargh attacks, the reason for the Tremen's suffering . . .'

Kest took a gulp of tea and coughed as he scalded his throat. 'Are you saying she would offer herself up to the Shargh to protect the Tremen?' The idea was appalling and difficult to believe, despite what he knew of her.

'Not *offer herself up* in the way you mean, although it might amount to the same thing.' Miken leaned forward. 'Kira lived and breathed for Kandor. Into him she poured all the love her mother didn't live to give her, and all the love her father wouldn't. Now that Kandor is gone, there's nothing left to hold her.'

'She has affection for Tresen,' pointed out Kest, as he struggled with Miken's revelations.

'That's constrained by clan-tie,' said Miken dismissively. 'Is there no one in the Warens she's shown interest in?'

He eyed Kest speculatively and Kest stared back. Did Miken suggest Kira could only be saved by bonding? *With him*? The idea was startling, but not without its attractions and well within Tremen law, despite them being bond-brother and sister. Miken was still intent on him, but he put the idea of bonding aside.

'Tresen, Werem, Paterek and Arlen are the only men who spend any time at all with her,' he said briskly. 'And, as you know, they're Kashclan. She heals, prepares pastes and potions, and records her knowing mainly alone. Eating and sleeping she does only when forced,' he added dryly, but the Kashclan leader's face remained heavy with worry, and Kest came to a decision. 'I won't tell Kira what we suspect about Bern's death,' he said. 'Instead, I'll emphasize the danger she'll put the Protectors in if she acts recklessly and remind her how essential her Healer skills are to all our futures. If, as you say, she puts others before herself, that should be enough.'

'For a while,' said Miken dourly.

Kira stomped around the mattress, taking out her frustration on the cavern floor. She had accorded Tresen the *courtesy* of informing him where she intended to go, *as a leader should*, and now all she got for her trouble was an argument. He perched on the chair someone had put in her alcove, probably to make it *homely,* and his reasonable tone added to her irritation.

'I don't think you should be going so far into the Warens on your own, and neither does Kest or else he wouldn't have left that advice with Protector Leader Pekrash.'

'The Protectors won't let me leave the Warens, and now you're saying I shouldn't even leave the training rooms. Maybe I should just sit here on my mattress and not move. Would that make you happy, Tresen?'

'I never said that and neither did Protector Leader Pekrash. It is advice, that's all. If you go off and get lost, then Protectors will have to search for you instead of protecting the longhouses.'

'Why in the 'green would I get lost? I've been to the Sarnia Room and back before.'

'Kest brought you back last time.'

'We came back together!' exclaimed Kira and plonked herself down on the mattress. 'I might go anyway. The Warens don't command the Bough.'

Tresen's eyes flashed. 'That sounds like something worthy of your father!' Kira faltered as the images of smoke and flames filled her head, and the mattress rustled as Tresen settled beside her. He pulled her close, his warm arms reassuring, and she shut her eyes and relaxed against him. 'I'm sorry. I didn't have the right to say that.'

'Maybe not,' she muttered. 'But it's true.'

He smoothed the hair from her face. 'Kira—'

The curtain was flicked back and Tresen scrambled to his feet and bowed to his Commander. Kest stared at them nonplussed. If it had been any other couple he would have sworn they were courting. 'Tremen Leader Kiraon, I was looking for you,' he said tightly, his eyes flicking between her and her stiffly standing clanmate.'

'Well, you have found me,' she said, barely looking at him.

Kest turned to Tresen. 'I've spent the last night at your longhouse, Protector. All is well there and Kashclanswoman Tenerini sends you some clothing. She also sends some for you, Tremen Leader Kiraon. I've left it in the outer cavern.'

'I thank you, Commander,' said Tresen.

Kest dismissed him with a nod, but Tresen glanced back to Kira as he left, and something indecipherable passed between them. Kest wondered again what he had interrupted. 'We need to speak,' he said.

Kira gestured to the chair, but Kest shook his head. A sleeping-room, even one as rudimentary as this one, was not an appropriate place for him to meet with the Tremen Leader. 'Where else in this cage would you suggest?' she demanded. Her eyes flashed gold and Kest suppressed a groan. He had thought they had developed a level of accord, but he was obviously mistaken.

'We can speak where you prepare the herbs,' said Kest.

'No, we will speak outside.' She scrambled to her feet and stood like a Protector about to start sword practice.

'As you wish.'

Her surprise was clear. 'You're letting me go outside?'

'As Tremen leader, you're free to go wherever you wish.'

Her eyes suffused with a goldy-green, the change astonishing, then she moved past him, and he followed her through the rows of wounded and out into the tunnel. From the back she looked like a child and he wondered how anyone so slight could hold such power.

'It's really a trick, isn't it, Protector Commander?' she said, glancing over her shoulder as she walked. 'I can only go where it's *responsible* to go; where I don't risk others.'

'You can describe it how you wish, Tremen Leader. If it's a trick, then it's one I'm caught by too. We are both obliged to put the Tremen before our personal wishes.'

There was an echo of marching feet and they stopped and drew close to the pitted wall as shadows snaked towards them. Merenor appeared through the murk at the head of patrol and Kest went forward to meet him. Merenor looked tired and pleased to be back, but the news was good: no new slashed trees and no sign of Shargh, despite the nearness to the full moon. Merenor finished his brief report and Kest clapped him on the shoulder and dismissed him.

'Where have they come from?' asked Kira, as the patrol's footfalls faded into the darkness.

'Renclan Octad.'

'Renclan? I thought the patrols concentrated on the north-eastern octads.'

'Not all.'

The map he had showed two Warens openings in Kenclan and one in Renclan, but he knew from his journey through the tunnels with Kira, that the map was not accurate. The Renclan and Kenclan octads shared the stone that produced the Sarnia caves and the underground stream, and being soft, was likely to have formed openings in Renclan. Having patrols in Renclan might dissuade the Shargh from searching for openings there but might also suggest there was something worth searching for.

'You have bad news for me, Protector Commander,' said Kira.

'What makes you think that?'

'Your face.'

'I was thinking of something else,' said Kest, and mentally cursed his lapse. It was the second time she had read him like a sheaf.

'So the news is good?'

By the 'green, she was persistent. 'We will speak of it outside, as you requested, Tremen Leader.'

Kira flicked back her braid and strode off across the last of the caverns, then jumped, as a figure stepped from the shadows. Only a Protector, praise the 'green, and obviously on entrance-guarding duty. Kest spoke to him briefly then dismissed him as he had dismissed Tresen earlier. How sure he was of himself. He had grown into his role of Protector Commander more quickly than she had grown into her role of leader. Then again, he had served as a Protector Leader before, while she had only gathered.

The sounds of the forest intruded, and Kira's heart quickened as she edged around Nogren, and stopped. Stinking heart-rot; it was dusk. For some reason, she had imagined it would be morning. Her journey to the clancouncil through the dew-bright forest of early morning had bequeathed her images of tippets and springleslips that had sustained her through the long days of writing, and she had expected to see them again now. Instead, the forest would soon be as dark as the Warens.

'You seem disappointed with your choice, Tremen Leader Kiraon.'

Kest's tone was mocking and she wondered if he smarted from her less-than-warm welcome earlier. 'The forest never disappoints me, Protector Commander. Even as day dies, bright-wings settle and silver moths rouse. Dusk is hunting time for the owls too, and for stickspiders to work their webs.' She ran her hand over Nogren's mighty trunk and peered up into its branches. 'When the moon rises, the canopy turns silver. Have you ever climbed to the top of an alwaysgreen, Protector Commander, and watched the canopy ripple like a vast silver ocean?'

'Not lately.'

'Shall we climb together?'

'Not tonight.'

'You disappoint me, Protector Commander. It seems I must climb alone.'

'We came to speak!'

'We can do so from the top of Nogren.'

Kest caught her arm. 'You're being foolish, Tremen Leader.'

'As long as I'm not being *irresponsible*, it doesn't matter.' She looked down at his hand on her arm. 'I'm a bit confused, Protector Commander. If I were to call for help now, would the Protectors aid me or you?'

Kest swore and dropped his hand. 'What's gotten into you, Kira? I thought at council you had stopped acting like a child.'

'Climb with me, Kest. I need to remember what I'm fighting for.'

Her eyes burned gold again, but there was no anger this time, just a strange combination of power and vulnerability. He swore again and tossed his sword at the base of the tree. 'I must be mad to even contemplate doing this,' he said, and followed her up.

15

Kira went quickly hand over hand, barely hesitating and never slipping but Kest went far more slowly. The tree's spiciness was overpowering and the foliage closer to the trunk than he remembered, or maybe he was a lot bigger than the last time he had climbed.

'Take care with the thinner branches,' he panted. They were already a considerable way up, and the thickening dusk meant Kira was barely visible above him. The return climb would be in complete darkness, he realized in dismay. He *was* mad!

'Don't worry, Protector Commander,' her voice floated down. 'No alwaysgreen has ever broken under a Kashclan climber.'

'I'm Morclan.'

'I'm sure they love Morclan too.'

He grinned despite himself but as the bole tapered and swayed, had to force himself not to look down. 'This is far enough,' he yelled.

'Only a little further.' He gritted his teeth and finally reached where she waited. 'Put your back to the tree and brace your feet there,' she said, as she pointed to a perch.

Kest gingerly maneuvered himself into place but she did not settle beside him, and Kest's heart jolted as she stepped away from him along the branch. 'Kira!'

'I just need to make a window,' she said. He saw the gleam of her teeth as she smiled. 'One slip and I become my namesake, the mira kiraon, except I can't fly.'

She was too far away for him to grab and his heart pounded as she balanced on the bough, and wove the foliage into an opening, then came nimbly back and settled on a nearby branch. 'Now you can see the canopy, Protector Commander, it's easy to imagine the mighty oceans of the north. *There our forebears landed, with the running horses of the far lands they once called home and, coming south, took the many-treed mountains and the plains for their own. And there they lived, loving both the forests and the plains, the speed of the running horse and the slow growth of herbs, until . . .*' She shrugged. 'Terak's blood-lust tore them apart and broke the first Kiraon's heart.'

'That was an act of stupidity,' gritted Kest, his neck slicked in a cold sweat.

'Kasheron would be insulted to hear you describe the record of his forebears' arrival thus.'

'I speak of *your* stupidity, not his. Why do you court death?'

'Perhaps death courts me. Tell me your news, Protector Commander.'

Kest took a steadying breath. 'Bern is dead.'

'Ah. Another I have killed.'

'You're a fool if you believe that,' he snapped. 'Bern told his father one thing and did another. He brought about his own death.'

Her eyes flashed in the first of the moonlight. '*No* boy of thirteen brings about his own death!'

Kest grimaced. Kandor was always there between Kira and those who might comfort her. How could the dead have so much power? 'You're right,' he conceded. 'In the past, it didn't matter that a boy loved to wander; that he told his father he was doing one thing, and did another, but those days are gone.' A breeze woke, and his perch swayed gently. It would have been pleasant had he not been so far off the ground.

'We can't survive this, Kest.'

'Hardly the words of a leader,' he said, and somehow managed to keep his tone even.

'Tell me what I say is untrue, Protector Commander.'

He forced a shrug. 'We don't know the Shargh's intent. They might tire of their sport and leave us in peace.'

'I've read many things in my search for fireweed, Protector Commander. The Shargh are hunters. They follow their prey on foot for days until they've killed whatever they seek.' Kest could think of nothing to say that was not a lie. 'Was it you who found Bern?' she asked.

'My patrol,' he said, and braced for her questions.

'Where was he?'

'Near the Kenclan Sentinel.' Now she would ask how he came to be so far from the Sarnia caves. The wind stirred again, and the leaves rustled.

'Did they cut his throat too?'

Kandor again; he should be grateful. 'No . . . he was stabbed.'

She said nothing for a long time and Kest shivered. His shirt was wet with sweat under his jacket and the breeze had freshened. 'Time to go.'

'I want to wait for moonrise.'

'Kira—'

'Please!'

Kest sighed. It seemed a small thing to ask. 'As you wish.' She said nothing more and in the silence that followed, he became aware of a myriad of small sounds: the creak of branches, the whisper of leaves, the scratching of small creatures above his head. In the distance, a bird gave voice, then another closer, and wings scythed the air.

'The hanawey hunts,' she said softly.

'And a frostking?'

'Perhaps. It sounded more like a hanawey hatchling. The parent bird and young often hunt together.'

'We see a lot of hanaweys on patrol. They are not as striking as the frostking, but quicker in flight. Which do you like best?'

'Neither.'

'Ah, let me guess. You favor the gold-eyed mira kiraon.'

'Yes, but not for its eyes; for its freedom.'

'Is it so bad in the Warens?'

'Kasheron never intended people to live there. He built the Bough to house healing and the longhouses to house the Tremen. The Warens were for storage and training.' Her branch rattled as she moved restlessly. 'I've finished the Writings, and Arlen and Paterek are more than halfway through the copies. Most of the wounded have gone back to their longhouses too. I pledged the council to remain only until they were all gone. I understand the Bough can't be rebuilt for the present, Kest, but I won't live my life in the Warens.'

Tendrils of moonlight drifted through the leaves painting her hair and skin silver. She was not the arrogant child of an arrogant leader, he had once supposed, nor a woman ready to bond as he had occasionally imagined, but something else, and Miken's warning of the dangers of her selflessness came back to him.

'You will be easier to protect, by my men, if you remain in the Warens,' he said carefully.

'The leader should endure the same hardships as the rest of the Tremen. I can hardly claim leadership if I skulk underground.'

'You wouldn't be *skulking*, you would be keeping healing safe and lessening the risk to the Protectors.'

Kira's branch jerked up and down. 'I've recorded my knowing and copies will soon be hidden around Allogrenia. Tresen or even Arlen or Paterek can heal as I do. Healing is safe regardless of what happens to me.'

'You know that isn't true. For one thing, no one else can take pain.' There was a short silence. 'I'm taking Protector Tresen back on patrol,' said Kest abruptly. He was keen to change the subject but that was not his only motivation. 'It's time he resumed his training, especially as the need for healing is less now, as you've pointed out.' Kira was silent but Kest pretended not to notice. He needed every man he could get on patrol, but he also wanted Tresen out of the Warens.

He knew of instances where clanmates broke Tremen law to take each other to their beds, or who had bonded multiple times, but never those of Kashclan. Kasheron's line adhered most strongly to his strictures but Kira's grief made her vulnerable and it was a grief Tresen shared. They also shared the closeness of a long friendship.

Clanleaders ensured breaches of Tremen law were not repeated, but as the Tremen Leader, Kira held authority over all the clanleaders, including Miken. A liaison between her and Tresen could tear the Tremen apart, and even if it did not, it had the potential to divide them *and* the Protectors along clan lines, and that was the last thing he needed. 'Miken will be glad to have his son back in his longhouse too,' he said, as the silence stretched. 'I know he's been missed there.'

'Yes, he's greatly loved.'

Her response was ambiguous, and Kest glanced at her sharply, but her face showed only sadness. His duty was to keep her safe, both from the Shargh *and* from breaking Tremen law, he reminded himself grimly. 'The moon's up,' he said with forced cheerfulness. 'Almost full. Very impressive.'

Kira followed his gaze but there was no pleasure in her face. 'It's a Shargh moon,' she said dully, 'a hunting moon.' She swung herself down from the branch. 'Time to go.'

The Sarnia Room produced equal feelings of excitement and dread, no matter how many times Kira visited it. What new remedies might lay hidden on its vast shelves of Writings? Cures for the aching bones of the old? Concoctions to stop a babe from coming early? Salves to replace the skin fire peeled away like sweetchew bark? Or tales of the Shargh and the Terak Kutan, and other scarcely guessed at barbaric peoples beyond the trees.

Searching through its sheafs was like searching the Drinkwater for glitterstones. Each Writing might contain something priceless on healing, but like the Drinkwater's treasures, might be buried under a vast detritus of duller stones, or in the Warens' case, under endless records of Allogrenia's administering.

At least she had plenty of time to search now, and no one she had to ask permission of. In ordering Tresen out of the Warens, Kest had lost his spy. She wondered if Kest had realized it yet. Tresen was sworn to obey his commander but the clan betrayal still rankled.

At least now he had gone, there was no one to argue with about going to the Sarnia Room or even deeper into the Warens, and no one to point out the *reasonableness* of Protector Leader Pekrash's commands.

Kira scowled as she thumped another sheaf down on the floor and flicked over the pages. How many times did the harvests of Allogrenia need to be recorded? And its births, and deaths, and bondings? *And* the goings-on of the Clancouncils? It must have been Kasheron's nature to want everything accounted for, and his sons had been record-keepers too, although they seemed to have tired of it after Kasheron's death. She had found nothing beyond season forty-three.

The meticulousness of Kasheron and his followers puzzled Kira. It seemed an unlikely trait in a people who had spent their lives riding, hunting, and fighting, and carving Allogrenia from the forest must have left little time, *or strength*, for other things.

She pushed the sheaf back onto the shelf and dusted herself down. Her clothes were grimy and her other set yet to be washed. Not that it mattered; there were few others in the Haelen to see *or* miss her. Arlen and Werem had gone gathering, and Paterek readied one of the wounded Sherclansmen for removal to his longhouse.

She wondered what Tresen was doing. Taking his midday meal with Miken and Tenerini perhaps? She could see the sunlit walls of the Kashclan longhouse and imagined him teasing Mikini across the table. Or perhaps he was on patrol through trees that now hid Shargh swords and daggers. She shivered. How she missed him! His jokes, his smiles, his easy familiarity. She never had to explain to him why she had chosen this herb over another, unlike with Arlen, Paterek and Werem.

Kesilini had gone as well, back to Morclan, and Kira missed her too because Kesilini was kind, and good-hearted, and *they had both loved Merek*. She shook her head savagely, angry the thought had intruded. She had no time for anything but finding some sort of weapon to use against the Shargh.

She wrenched another sheaf from the shelf, sneezed repeatedly in the dust, and cursed as she discovered still more records. Nothing on the Shargh, or on the battles the Northerners fought, nothing of any use at all.

She struggled to her feet and surveyed the shelves opposite. Perhaps she would start there, even though the sheafs looked newer. She chose one at random but as she slid it off the shelf, pages fluttered down like leaves all over the cavern floor. Stinking heart-rot! The sheafs must be older than they looked, and the stitching decayed. Now she would have to spend valuable reading time putting it all back together again.

She knelt on the dusty floor. They were not Writings at all, but maps like the one of the Warens she had found but Kest had taken. She peered down at them. They were not just of the Warens either, *or* of Allogrenia, but of other lands. Her hands shook as she picked one up. There were settlements marked on it with strange and exotic names: *Kessom, Maraschin, Talliel*, words she rolled around in her mouth like food. One map even had an ocean called the *Oskinas*.

She selected another headed *Allogrenia and lands*. The floor bit into her knees but she scarcely noticed. It showed the lands west, north, and east of Allogrenia, and as her eyes darted over it, the flowing script resolved itself into a familiar word: *Shargh*. Even in the safety of the cavern, the word had the power to make her tremble. Their lands were So close! Only a little north-east of the Kenclan Sentinel where Bern had been killed.

She chewed her lip. It did not make sense. The Sentinel was a long way from the Sarnia caves. Perhaps the distances were not the same. What had Kest called such things? *Scane*? *Scale*? Yet the Eights seemed to be in the right position compared to other things, evenly spaced, a day's march apart. She settled on her backside and hugged her knees.

Why had Bern gone to the Sentinel anyway? It was nearly a three-day trek from where she had seen him, and he had been excited about exploring the caves. And then for some reason, he had gone off to the Sentinel *or been taken*!

She shuddered at the thought of him being dragged, terrified, through the trees. But why had the Shargh take him all the way to the Sentinel when they could have killed him where they found him? She stared down at the map. It looked about a two-day walk from the Sentinel to the Shargh lands. Maybe they had intended to take him to their lands but got tired of his struggles. But why take him there anyway? The Shargh came to kill not kidnap?

She pushed a grimy hand through her hair. She was tired of asking questions that had no answers. She gathered the maps and returned them to the shelf. The third shelf down, fifth section from the entranceway, she noted. She made her way back to the tunnel, extinguished the lamp and placed it just inside the cavern, and set off into the darkness.

16

Kira's thoughts returned to Kest as she walked. Her *bond-brother* would not be happy. The topic of their very first conversation had been her *not* wandering in the Warens and it had been the topic of countless ones since, along with her *not* being irresponsible, *not* being childish, and *not* risking healing.

But it was hard to be angry with him. His care for Allogrenia and for those he commanded was etched into his face. When was the last time she had seen him smile? After she had delivered Feseren's son? He had been happy then, his eyes sky-blue, not the blank grey they often were now. How grim he had been in Nogren when he had told her of Bern's death.

The stone disappeared under her fingertips and her hand sailed into nothingness: the first left turning. They were two more, roughly two hundred paces apart, before the tunnel swung west to join one of the better-used tunnels.

She concentrated on counting her steps and allowed herself a small smile each time the stone gave way and her memory was confirmed. She wondered how many others had found their way by touch, here in darkness, or walked this way by lamplight. Tremen Protectors certainly, but who else?

Had people lived in the forests before Kasheron and his followers? The sheafs did not speak of anyone, nor did the Tremen, but that didn't prove anything. She had learned many things over the past moons that no one spoke of and there was probably a lot more only the Protectors knew.

The walls whispered with voices, and she stopped, nerves tingling. The main tunnel must be close, but sound traveled strangely in the Warens and the speakers could be distant. Wherever they were, they were a long way from the training rooms and from Nogren. She frowned. The Protectors mainly guarded the longhouses now, except for the patrols in Renclan and Kenclan, Kest had mentioned.

Perhaps he had sent a patrol into the Warens to test the map she had found. She did not want to meet them in her present grubby state or run into Kest either, deep in the Warens, *on her own*, without lamp. She would wait to see whether the speakers came her way, and if they did, follow quietly along behind.

When she reached the main tunnel, she took several steps back and settled on the floor to wait. The voices ebbed and flowed, but no one appeared, and she hugged her knees for warmth. She was thirsty too, having forgotten to bring a waterskin. Curse this waiting. She wanted to get back to her alcove, wash and have a very long drink. Maybe the men she heard were already back in the training rooms and she was sitting here in the dark like a fool.

She struggled to her feet but then the rasp of boots was suddenly very close, and the voices resolved into individual words. '. . . *sleep in a decent bed . . .*' '. . . *old enough to know better, still, you can't tell a Morclansman anything . . .*' '. . . *best ale I've had . . .*' '. . . *since the last one . . .*' someone chipped in. There was a grunt of laughter and Kira grinned. A glow appeared then elongated shadows that snaked along in advance of their owners, and then the first of the Protectors passed her line of vision.

The tunnel was narrow here and they were strung out. She did not recognize the Protector Leader and those nearest him held their silence, but the conversations picked up toward the rear of the patrol. '. . . *heartily sick of this darkness . . .*' someone grumbled. So am I, thought Kira. '. . . *not a place you'd want to live . . .*'

'*At least she's safe here,*' a second voice broke in, and Kira stiffened.

'. . . *not safe anywhere, anymore,*' the first speaker said. '*There's an opening in Renclan, and two in Kenclan, and who's to say there aren't more. And the cursed Shargh would know all about Nogren, after what they did to Bern. Poor Bern . . .*'

There was a shout from the Leader ordering them back into formation, a rapid staccato of feet as the men complied, and the echo of their passing faded, to leave a faint smell of lamp oil on the dank air. Kira remained frozen against the wall as everything became appallingly clear. Bern had been taken to the edge of the forest to force information from him about *her*.

The Shargh did not speak Tremen, so they must have had someone with them who did it, or Terak, which was the same anyway. Bern had been stabbed, Kest said, and now she knew why. Cutting his throat would have been too quick. By the alwaysgreen that Sheltered them! They had tortured him because of *her*.

Her knees gave way and she slid down the wall. Kest knew what the Shargh had done to Bern and why, or else how did the Protectors know? The Shargh did not hunt *healing* they hunted *her*! And Kest sent patrols through the Warens in search of other entry points, not to keep *healing* safe, but to keep *her* safe.

But the Protectors were right; there *was* no safety. Sooner or later, the Shargh would find a way in, hunt her down in the darkness, and kill her. And how many others would die too? How many other *Berns*? How many other *Kandors*?

Vomit spilled from her mouth and she rocked on her knees as tears mixed with the liquid on the floor, and then she rolled away from it and lay curled in the darkness. Her very existence put every Tremen at risk. Surely her death would be better?

Death came to everyone and everything, even the alwaysgreens fell to give their essence back to the earth so new things might grow. It was not death she feared but the moment of death: the slice of the blade through her flesh, the blood in her lungs, the pain. Her face grew wet with tears again and she dashed them away. She was a coward huddling here in the darkness feeling sorry for herself.

She dried her face on her shirt and hauled herself upright. Kest might not have lied outright but he had hidden the truth, and it amounted to the same thing. And Tresen had *hidden the truth* too. Who else knew apart from the Protectors? Miken? Was she to live her life surrounded by liars? Maybe the Shargh *did* hunt healing and in their eyes, she and healing were the same but then why leave the Kashclan longhouse alone? They probably knew from Bern healing was strong there.

And there had been no attacks for two moons, which suggested they *were* after her, not healing. Or maybe they wanted to destroy the Tremen Leadership, not her in particular, but it amounted to the same thing. Maybe, maybe! Maybe she was desperate for an explanation that did not include her death!

Whichever way she looked at it, her choices were horrifyingly clear: stay in the Warens until the Shargh inevitably found her or leave Allogrenia. There would be a lot of killing if she stayed. Kest would sacrifice every last Protector, including himself, before he surrendered her. And if she left?

She had a terrifying vision of running through the trees pursued by the pound of Shargh feet, and the flash of metal in sunlight. Would the Shargh leave the Tremen in peace once she was dead? If she knew the answer to that question, her decision would be simpler.

She forced her feet forward, having to use the wall as a support as well as a guide. Was there no other choice? The map had shown other places with other peoples beyond the trees. Perhaps they would help. But why should they?

What were the Tremen to them? Did they even know of the Tremen's existence? Kasheron had hidden them too well. The trees that had sheltered them from possible enemies, had sheltered them from possible friends. The only peoples who knew of their existence were the Terak Kutan.

She stopped. The Terak Kutan were kin, blood-linked, and so obliged to offer aid, but to go begging to them betrayed everything Kasheron had fought for. It would be healing bending its knee to the sword. It was abhorrent! Unthinkable! There must be another way! Once she had eaten and rested, and perhaps spoken with Kest or Miken, things would not seem so bleak. And there were many Writings yet to be read that might reveal other forms of aid.

Powerful salves to make the Shargh disappear? Potions to unburn the Bough? Tinctures to bring the dead to life again? She shook her head, silencing the mocking voice. Food and sleep was what she needed, and time to think.

Pain was the same whether it was the pain of a birthing woman, a turned ankle, or a sword wound. Under Kira's fingers, in the flame-filled world Feseren had shown her, it always wore the same face. Now as she ran her fingers over the partly-healed wound, pain smiled its ghastly smile, though the young Protector's face remained unchanged. 'Does it hurt here?' she asked. Brithin shook his head. 'Here?' Her fingers burned, but again the head shake.

Kira flicked her fingers to dispel the heat, glad her only witness was a young Protector keen to escape the Warens. Even if he noticed, he would not understand what he saw, not that she understood her sensitivity to pain either.

'Another few days,' she said, and eased his shirt back over his shoulder.

Brithin's disappointment was clear. 'The wound feels well. I'm strong enough to go.'

She buttoned his shirt, its buttons made of sever like the ones on Kandor's shirts. Pain burned again. 'Clanleader Tenedren has enough to do with guarding your longhouse without worrying about you,' she snapped, as she gathered her salves. His face fell, and Kira took a deep breath. He was the last of the wounded; it was understandable he wanted to join his clanmates.

'When Arlen comes back, I'll ask him to help you take some gentle exercise to build your strength,' she said. He nodded, and Kira went to the table at the side, crushed morning-bright into a bowl of hot water, and smelled the air sweeten. The vapors should soothe Brithin's impatience, she thought, as she picked her way through the empty mattresses to her alcove.

The Haelen seemed cavernous without its rows of wounded, the neatly folded covers atop each mattress testament to her work here being all but done. The alcove was the same though, small and dingy, and she tossed the salves on her mattress and wandered restlessly around the cramped space. Maybe she should go back and inhale the morning-bright leaves herself!

It remained quiet in the Haelen and she peered through the crack in the curtain, then lifted the mattress, its sere grass stuffing rustling as she drew out a map. She did not unfold it but half-closed her eyes and visualized the route through the Warens that would exit her close to the Renclan Second Eight. Only then did she examine the map and give a satisfied grin.

Her memory of the way was accurate, which meant the map could go back to the Sarnia Room, safe from the Shargh. She would rehearse the route regularly to keep it fresh in her mind. She slid the first map back into its hiding place and drew out the second one. It showed the lands north of Allogrenia and all the way to the Oskinas Sea, and her hands trembled as she unfolded it. She was not going to try to memorize it; she was taking a copy with her. The Shargh would already know the north so it would not matter if they got hold of it.

Kira was not sure when her resolve to leave Allogrenia had crystallized, but it was there now, as hard as sun-baked sap. But she did not know what she would do afterwards, *if* she somehow escaped the Shargh's blades. Seeking aid from the Terak Kutan remained abhorrent. Every Writing she had come across described their blood-thirst, or their brutality, or their utter contempt of healing. Her stomach knotted but surely Terak, who like his brother Kasheron had been birthed by the great Healer Queen, Kiraon, must have carried *some* love of healing he had passed on down his line.

143

But whatever the Terak Kutan's true natures, they were a long way north. She stared at the rivers and mountains on the map in horrified fascination. She would have to cross them all *and* carry enough food for the journey. Her pack was not big, especially with her Healer's kit, and she considered what she could forage before she left Allogrenia.

The map of the Warens showed an opening near the Second Eight in Renclan, and there were two openings in Kenclan, but she needed to go north, not north-east towards the Shargh's lands. She frowned thoughtfully.

If she exited the Warens beyond the Second Eight, it was three days to the Renclan Sentinel, and the gathering in Renclan was plentiful. The map showed a plain at the edge of the forests, the *Dendora*. It looked lightly treed, *if* the blotches of ink represented trees, and some of them should be blacknuts. Even if they were not, there should be pitchie seeds, which she had read Kasheron's folk relied on.

Unlike many of the other features on the map, the Dendora Plain was not followed by an 'S' or 'T'. Kira guessed that mountains, plains, and rivers with two names followed by 'S' or 'T' denoted Shargh and Terak names for the same thing, although there could be other peoples whose names started with 'S' and 'T'. Onespeak was the result of diverse peoples needing to communicate but seeing evidence of it on the map was extraordinary.

The Dendora Plain lay west of the Shargh lands and she hoped the absence of an 'S' meant the Shargh didn't go there, but the massive mountain range she must cross *if* she went north, did have two names: *Azurcades* followed by 'T', and *Braghans*, followed by 'S' and *if* the map were to scale, it looked like an eight-day trek across the Dendora

Plain to the Braghans-Azurcades.

Eight days of out-running the Shargh, a hunting people, who followed their prey to its death, and *then* she must climb a massive mountain range they probably frequented too. Cold sweat oozed down her back. It would be better to stay in the Warens, to hide in the darkness, to seek out the most obscure cavern and spend her life there. The Shargh would never find her, it would be safe, no one would know . . .

She scrambled to her feet and paced up and down. If she stayed in Allogrenia, Tremen would die. She knew it and Kest probably did too. If she were to be a leader in more than name, she must leave, not just to tempt the Shargh to follow her, but to seek aid.

She brought a shaking hand to her mouth as the reality of what she must do settled over her. She must go north and demand the Terak Kutan honor the blood-link. *Demand*? She swallowed dryly. She was a fool if she believed she was in a position to do other than beg.

The Tremen had no love for the Terak Kutan and for the first time she considered what the Terak Kutan thought of them. Probably the same, she conceded, given no Terak Kutan had come south to see how the other half of their people fared. She smiled sourly. Given she was unlikely to live long enough to leave Allogrenia, she had no reason to worry.

17

Kira stared at the dull wink of crystal in the stone, reminded abruptly of when she had woken in the Warens after the first attack. It was like looking back at someone else entirely, a Kira who no longer existed. She half shrugged and dragged her attention back to the map.

Just suppose, by some extraordinary chance, the Shargh *did not* catch her, and there were nuts or other forage on the Dendora Plain. How was she to cross the Braghans? The *Azurcades*, she corrected. She would not use the Shargh word, *if* it were a Shargh word!

The Azurcades seemed to be treed as well, so there would be shelter and possibly nuts, and maybe scavenger leaf or pitchie seeds, but there might also be many days of climbing, and cliffs, and maybe rushing rivers. She had no idea if people lived there either, and if they did, whether they would be friends or enemies.

And *if* she survived the Azurcades, there was a second plain on the northern side, far bigger than the Dendora, called the *Sarsalin*. She calculated the distance. Another ten days of journeying to cross *it* if all went well.

She wiped her sweaty palms on her trousers. Looking so far ahead was like watching a heart-rotted tree crash towards her. All she could do was take each day as it came. First she needed to reach the Fourth Eight, then the Sentinel, then survive the first day on the Dendora, then survive the second.

'Leader Kiraon?'

She started violently. Kest's outline was visible on the other side of the curtain. 'One moment, Commander,' she called, quickly folding the map, and sliding it under the mattress. The sere grass stuffing rustled again, and she hoped Kest would think it related to some private female matter. He had developed an irritating sense of proprietary recently, refusing to come into her alcove, which at least had saved her from discovery.

Kest looked fresh and relaxed: his face lightly tanned, his eyes a startling blue despite the dim light. He even smelled of sun-tinged air and Kira smoothed down her crumpled over-sized Protector shirt, aware of how unkempt she must look. Her other clothes were a better fit, but they still dried near the very small fire the vents allowed.

'Only one wounded remains, I see,' he said, glancing back at the Haelen.

'Yes, Brithin of Kenclan. There's still pain in the wound, so it's best he stays here until it fades.'

'Is that his view too?' asked Kest with a smile.

Kira shrugged. 'He's young. It's natural he misses his clan-kin and fellow Protectors.'

'He's nineteen Kira. Two seasons older than you.'

Kest's face had gentled and she shifted uncomfortably. 'I'm sure you didn't come here to discuss my age, Protector Commander.'

'No, I came here to see how you were,' he said, still smiling.

'I am well, as you can see.'

'What I see is someone who is too thin and too pale.'

'Ah, I see you've learned healing since last we spoke,' she said.

Kest's smile stayed firmly in place. 'I think it would be good for you to go to the Kashclan longhouse for a time.'

Kira blinked in astonishment. She must really look awful. 'I still have a wounded man here to care for.'

'Then go after he departs. A few more days, you said.' He glanced around. 'Come to the second training room, Kira. It's a pleasanter place to talk and we can eat there as well.'

'I prefer Nogren,' said Kira. His hand closed over her arm in the same way she held the injured as they took their first steps, but while she *supported* the wounded, he *directed* her, and she had to resist the urge to shrug him off.

'My turn to choose,' said Kest lightly, as he steered her through the mattresses.

He was in a good mood which she was loath to ruin, but she needed to test her theory. 'I've been thinking about everything that's happened,' she began, as they entered the tunnel. 'I think there's a pattern to the Shargh's attacks.'

The passed a lamp and its light revealed that Kest's face had become guarded. 'What mean you?' he said.

'The Shargh ignored the longhouses in their journey to the Bough, and they killed Bern because he wandered alone. I think they mistook him for a Healer out gathering. I think they want to destroy healing.' Their footsteps echoed hollowly in the silence that followed, and the next lamp showed Kest's expression had eased again. 'Do you believe they killed Bern because they thought he was a Healer?' she asked. Thank the 'green it was some way to the next lamp so Kest could not see *her* face.

She felt the tension in his hand increase. 'It is possible,' he said.

'If I go to the Kashclan longhouse, it might suggest it's a place of healing. I don't want to risk those there,' she said, and felt his fingers relax. 'Do you believe I am right Protector Commander?'

'You could be.'

'I value *your* opinion, Protector Commander. Do *you* believe it?' What he said now almost determined whether she stayed or went. If she could not trust Kest to tell her the truth, there was no point remaining in Allogrenia.

He was a long time answering and she held her breath. 'Yes,' he said finally. Kira staggered and his grip tightened again. 'Are you unwell?' he asked in alarm.

They came to another lamp and she turned her face away. 'Just a little tired.' Tired of the darkness and dankness and dust; of being old enough to lead but not old enough to hear the unpalatable truth; of being afraid, but most of all, of being alone.

The second training room was bright with lamps and full of Protectors lately come in off patrol. They spoke noisily and joked as they shared plates of nutbread and sweetfish, and steaming cups of thornyflower tea.

The hubbub quieted slightly as Kest and Kira passed, but soon picked up again. Pekrash and Merenor were there, sitting with Protector Leaders Kira did not know, and Kest guided her to their table. They stood to greet her. 'Protector Leaders Merenor and Pekrash I believe you know,' said Kest, 'and this is Protector Leader Senden of Kenclan, and Protector Leader Bendrash of Sherclan.'

'Kashclan greets Kenclan and Sherclan,' said Kira, with a bow. She did not know whether the usual clan greeting was appropriate between a Tremen Leader and a Protector Leader, but she was more concerned with her baggy Protector shirt and her unraveling braid. Like Kest, the Protector Leaders were neat and fresh-looking.

'We would be pleased for you to join us,' said Pekrash, with a small bow.

'I thank you,' said Kest smoothly, before Kira could reply, 'but the Tremen Leader and I have matters to discuss.'

Kest still had hold of her arm and she ground her teeth as he steered her to a table in the furthest corner. 'I'll get us some food,' he said, as soon as she was seated, and headed back into the throng. Kira glanced back at the Protector Leaders, their faces sombre as they spoke together. They knew what Kest knew, as the young Protectors opposite probably did. In fact, everyone in the room probably knew about the threat to her, and possibly other things denied the *Tremen Leader.*

One of the young Protectors nearby caught her eye, and he glanced towards Kest, who had been accosted by a weary-looking older man, then made his way over. 'Tremen Leader Kiraon,' he said, bowing low, and catching her hands.

Kira went to rise but his grip on her hands made movement awkward. 'Protector . . .?'

'Protector Arin of Tarclan,' he said hurriedly, his gaze flicking to Kest again.

'Kashclan greets Tarclan,' said Kira automatically, wondering if Arin were about to tell her something Kest did not want her to know.

'Tremen Leader . . . I wish to thank you for saving my brother, Eresh.' Arin's eyes glistened and he bowed again.

'I am a Healer, Protector Arin, there's no need for thanks.'

His head bobbed again and his grip on her hands tightened. 'Eresh said you healed his pain. He said—' Arin's eyes went to Kest again, who headed in their direction and Kira took the opportunity to extricate her hands.

'I thank you for your words, Arin.'

Arin straightened, and with a final bow made his way back to his comrades, bowing again to Kest as they passed. 'What did Protector Arin of Tarclan have to say for himself?' asked Kest, as he juggled a platter of nutbread, sweetfish and sour-ripe onto the table, followed by cups of thornyflower tea.

Normally Kira would have found the enquiry innocent, but now she found it intrusive. Did Kest think Arin had told her something she was not allowed to know? That the Shargh hunted *her*, not healing?

'He thanked me for healing his brother,' she muttered, and took a sip of her tea.

'Protector Eresh,' said Kest thoughtfully. 'He was one I didn't think would survive, and he wouldn't have, had you not found the fireweed.' His voice was gentle, and he clearly intended his words as a compliment, but Kira kept her eyes on the table. There was a short silence and she heard his fingers tap. It never took Kest long to become irritated with her. 'Aren't you going to eat?' he asked.

'I'm not hungry.'

'When was the last time you did eat?' Kira shrugged, and he seized her wrist and pushed her cuff up. 'All bone and no flesh, Kira! Is that how a Healer looks after herself?'

'Don't!' She tried to wrench herself free, but he was as angry too, and his grip tightened.

'Then eat,' he said, and released her. His eyes were like ice. 'If you sicken, who will heal? You don't have the right—'

'Don't lecture me on rights! The healing is recorded, Protector Commander. There's a copy in the training room, three deep in the Warens, one in the Tarclan longhouse, one in the Sherclan longhouse. Tresen is a gifted Healer,

151

Brem is good; Werem, Arlen and Paterek improving. *You* don't need me anymore, Protector Commander; the *Tremen* don't need me anymore!'

He leaned across the table. 'What are you talking about?' She shrugged, picked up a piece of nutbread, and took a bite to appease him. 'You will always be needed, Kira. You're the Tremen Leader. Even if, *when* this is over, when the stinking Shargh have gone, you will be needed.'

Kira swallowed the moist lump of nutbread and managed to look up. 'Tell me, Kest, is it the task of the Tremen Leader to save the Tremen people?'

His eyes narrowed. 'By healing?'

Kira nodded. 'By stopping their suffering.'

Kest's gaze on her face was intense, as if he searched for hidden meanings. 'Of course,' he said finally. 'Why do you ask?'

'Sometimes in the Warens, I need reminding, that's all.' She forced a smile. 'It is easy to forget in the darkness.'

18

The day was dying, flutterwings spiraling to the forest floor, the canopy all but empty of birdsong. Kest scarcely noticed. He was so preoccupied that he only became aware of his proximity to the Kashclan longhouse when he was challenged by a Protector patrol.

He should be on his way to his own longhouse for some much-needed sleep, before he met with the Protector Leaders for the patrols' reports, but he needed to speak with Miken. Kest had spent four days in Kenclan octad with Senden's patrol, and another two journeying back through Renclan. No wonder his bones ached.

He had walked further in the few last moons than he had in the previous twelve, but at least the news was good. The third full moon since the last attack had passed and the night forest grew dim again and there were no more slashed trees, no Tremen unaccounted for, and no Shargh sightings. He knew better than to believe the Shargh had gone away. They waited, but for what?

His thoughts turned to Kira. Perhaps it was his concern for her, not for the Shargh, that fed his unease. It had been many days since her eyes had flashed that extraordinary rebellious gold, but she seemed even less in accord with him than before.

At that age Kesilini had been cool when he had upset her, and overly loving when he had pleased her. But Kira was not like Kesilini, or any other woman he had ever known. If anything, she was more like an enthusiastic young Protector whose exuberance must be usefully channeled, and whose dangerous inclinations must be curtailed.

High in Nogren's branches, she had been as wild as a bird, her eyes smoldering as she had walked out on the branch. Cold sweat beaded his brow even at the memory. Her recklessness hinted at some sort of death wish, and he wondered whether it stemmed from the loss of her family, or whether it had always been part of her nature. He had not known her before the Shargh attacks and most of those who had were dead, except for Miken *and* Tresen, which was why he was here and not in his bed.

Miken's longhouse was beautifully carved, but even as a Morclansman, Kest did not pause to admire it, just strode up the path and rapped on the door. It swung open almost immediately to reveal Tresen. The young Protector's surprise was clear, but he recovered quickly to bow. 'Commander Kest . . . I . . . Kashclan welcomes Morclan.'

'Morclan thanks Kashclan,' replied Kest. 'Is your father within?'

'He's beyond the Second Eight gathering with a patrol. Please come in.' Kest's thoughts raced and he stayed where he was. If Miken was beyond the Second Eight, he would not be back before the morrow. 'Would you like me to send a message to him to return?' asked Tresen.

'No. I . . .' Kest stopped. He had wanted Miken to confirm his fears for Kira's well-being were sound, that Tresen and Kira together in the Warens would not risk them breaching Tremen law on clanmates bonding, and that removing Tresen from the Warens, and then sending him back, wasn't the mark of a weak and indecisive leader. But now, it seemed, he would have to think for himself.

'I know you are on leave, Protector Tresen, but I have a favor to ask.'

'By all means, Commander. But please, come in and eat with us first.'

Kest peered past him to where Kashclan took their evening meal. The smell of new-baked nutbread made his mouth water but he shook his head. 'I thank you, Protector Tresen, but I must be back in my own longhouse before dawn.' He lowered his voice. 'Who commands the Kashclan guard in Miken's absence?'

'Farion.'

'I will request he releases you. I want you to return to the Warens. Call it Healer duty, if you wish, but I want someone with the Tremen Leader.'

Tresen's eyes narrowed. 'I thought Kesilini was there.'

'Kesilini's been back in the Morclan longhouse since before the last moon and the training room is all but empty of wounded. Arlen and Paterek are there, of course, and I know that Kira spends time sorting the sheafs in the Sarnia Room, but the Warens can be a lonely place. The council must soon decide when and how to rebuild the Bough. In the meantime, I would feel better if she had the company of someone who knew her before this began.'

'I will leave at dawn,' said Tresen.

'I would prefer you went now.'

'I will go immediately, Commander.'

'Thank you, Protector. I will be in Renclan octad with Clanleader Sanden for the next few days but back in the Warens by the new moon. We can discuss your duties more fully then.'

155

The new sun glanced off the sorchas' eastern walls and sent the spur's shadow sliding to where the ebis still slumbered, legs rigid legs, heads low. In the highest sorcha on the spur, Palansa did not sleep, her aching back and the sorcha's stifling air ensuring she stayed wakeful. Ormadon insisted the sorcha's flaps be shut when they slept, but the air pooled like the scum-filled puddles in the Thanawah, and Palansa's shift stuck to her back and breasts, and plastered her hair across her forehead.

In the end, she struggled from the bed, and loosed a flap. The dawn air was scarcely any fresher but she stayed by the vent, rocking from side to side on swollen feet, and rubbing her back as she stared across the Grounds. The air was already heavy with the smell of dust and dry grass, and soon the ebis would shamble towards the Thanawah in ragged lines, tails aflick at the blackflies.

She turned so that her gaze followed the slope beyond the cave of the Tellers and Cashgars, to the distant blue of the Braghans, until the press of her belly against the wall prevented her seeing further. She was tighter than a drum and a lot heavier, but at least the babe was quiet now after kicking the entire night! She considered returning to bed to snatch some more sleep, but pain jabbed, and she paced instead, knowing the pain grew less when she walked.

She navigated her way around the sorcha, taking care not to nudge or kick anything that might disturb Tarkenda. Two days earlier, the older woman had lain her rough hands over Palansa's belly and pronounced the next chief ready to be born, then she had fetched some sweet-oil and rubbed Palansa's back. Palansa had slept, and when she had woken, the swaddlings Tarkenda had used with Erboran and Arkendrin had been set by the bed, and a sleep-sling for the babe fastened to the roof.

156

None of it seemed real, thought Palansa, as she linked her hands under the mountain of her shift. The babe that had flickered inside her as light as button-flower seed, now bulged her belly with foot and fist, and would soon be in her arms. Erboran's son; she smiled and then gasped as new pain speared.

'What is it?' asked Tarkenda, coming awake.

'Just my back,' said Palansa. She lowered herself onto a stool and screwed her eyes shut as the pain grew.

Tarkenda sat up and tucked her hair back into her grizzled plait. 'I'll rub it for you.' Palansa heard the uneven pad of Tarkenda's feet across the pelts and the clunk of wood hitting wood as she retrieved the oil from the basket of ease-pots. 'Come and lie down.'

Palansa heaved herself up and was engulfed in a wave of nausea. She retched and clung to the table. 'My back is making me ill,' she muttered.

Tarkenda peered at her. 'I think the babe comes.'

Palansa retched again and Tarkenda fetched a bowl, helped Palansa onto the bed, and then ducked out through the door flap. Outside, the air was thick with blackflies, but the spur was still quiet. Ormadon leaned on his spear as he surveyed the slope.

'There's a storm coming, Chief-mother.'

Tarkenda followed his gaze towards the Braghans. The sky was clear, but she felt the same faint tingling. 'Has Arkendrin returned?'

'No, Chief-mother, nor those who keep him company. Most of the lower sorchas are empty.' Ormadon's black eyes held hers. 'Since the moons of mourning finished, his followers course north and east of the forests, where Irdodun first saw the Healer, and where she escaped

Arkendrin before. The treemen now favor these reaches too. Arkendrin knows time grows short.'

'Shorter than he thinks. Palansa's taken to her bed.'

The furrows of Ormadon's face deepened. 'Then it's better he isn't here, Chief-mother. Will the Chief-wife birth this day?'

'I don't think so. I labored two dawns to birth Erboran, and a babe will often follow its father in such things.'

Ormadon turned the spear over in his hands, as if he tested its strength. 'I will summon those loyal to the blood-born chief to ensure the Chief-wife births in peace. And I will tell Gensana to start her baking. The Sky Chiefs will have their squaziseed and shillyflower cakes to keep them content.' His face broke into a smile. 'It will be good to have a chief in the highest sorcha again, even if he does squall.'

A long, shuddering groan sounded from the sorcha and he touched his brow and stared skyward. 'May the Sky Chiefs send her strength.'

'And a cool day,' added Tarkenda.

Tresen let fall the curtain to Kira's alcove, and rubbed his sweaty brow. He had journeyed fast through the night, spurred on by the thought of sharing a hot thornyflower tea and fresh nutbread with her, but he had been greeted by an empty alcove and a solitary water jug. Kest had not hidden his anxiety about Kira, and Tresen had half feared he would find her silent and hunched in a corner. But it would have been unlike her. Kira was never still where there was healing to be administered or Writings on it to be explored.

She was probably in the Sarnia Room with her nose buried in a dusty sheaf, but Kest's worry had infected him, and he wanted to make sure she *was* well. He wandered back into the Haelen, filled a cup from a water jug on the side table, and drank. The water was halfway down his throat before the dank taste hit him and he grimaced and set the cup down.

A few days back in his longhouse, or on patrol under the rustling leaves, was enough to forget how bleak the Warens were, except Kira never had the chance to forget. Apart from her fireweed expedition and the clancouncils, she had been in the Warens since he and Miken had carried her there, senseless with grief and terror. It seemed a long time ago now.

Footsteps echoed, the unmistakable tread of Protectors marching, and he tensed as an order was shouted and they halted outside the cavern. By the 'green; he hoped it didn't herald more wounded. A set of footsteps detached itself and Tresen turned to see Penedrin, the Protector Leader's face weary and sweat-stained. 'Leader Kiraon is here?' he asked.

Tresen shook his head, the Protector Leader's lack of greeting adding to his tension. 'I've just arrived myself on Commander Kest's orders. I assume the leader is in the Sarnia Room. Have you wounded with you?'

Penedrin turned back to the tunnel and barked an order, Tresen heard the patrol march on, then Penedrin returned. 'I've sent the patrol to the Sarnia Room. We must know exactly where the leader is. There are newly slashed trees in the Renclan octad. I returned via the Renclan longhouse and Commander Kest takes a patrol north now. If the leader returns or you learn of her whereabouts, send a message to me *immediately* at the Sarnia Room.' He nodded briefly and strode out.

Tresen's heart thundered. Renclan had only one opening to the Warens, but the Shargh might still find their way in, and if they did . . . There was the soft fall of footsteps and he whirled in relief, but it was Arlen, the Kashclansman's face reflecting Tresen's surprise but not his disappointment. 'Tresen! Welcome. I didn't expect to see you here.'

'Why not?'

'Well, I thought you would be guarding our longhouse, as the leader is there.'

'What makes you think the leader's at Kashclan?'

'I . . . I assumed it was so,' said Arlen, taken aback. 'The Protectors said she would go there when the last of the wounded went home, so when Brithin was taken and the leader left, I thought that's where she had gone.'

'*Left*? When did you last see her?'

Arlen stood considering with maddening slowness. 'It must be nearly two days,' he said, 'though it's hard to track time here.'

'And you didn't think to tell anyone? Stinking heart-rot, Arlen! She could be lying injured in the Warens!' *Or already in Shargh hands*.

Arlen looked startled. 'She hasn't gone into the Warens, Tresen.'

'What makes you so sure?'

'She took her clothing and a sword.'

Tresen gaped at him. '*A sword*?'

'She came to the training rooms and asked for one,' explained Arlen. 'Paterek sharpened a practice sword for her. They're lighter. I . . . *we* assumed she would carry one since she was going back under the trees.'

Tresen rushed back to the alcove, Arlen close behind him. Her pack was gone, but she always carried it anyway,

160

and she owned so little it was impossible to tell whether anything else was missing. He gazed about wildly. The bed was neat, the cover pulled smooth, but there was a sprig of something on it he had not noticed before and he snatched it up.

'Cinna,' said Arlen helpfully. 'It must have fallen from her pack.'

'Herbs don't *fall* from Kira's pack,' snapped Tresen, his thoughts bubbling. Why in the 'green had she left it? Cinna was the first herb to poke its leaves through the leaf-litter in spring, and the last to die away. The clans hung it in their longhouses in winter as a reminder that spring would come again. There was even a children's rhyme about it: *Silvermint to calm, bluemint to smooth the scar, icemint to balm, cinna to remember.*

He seized Arlen's arm. 'Send message to Penedrin in the Sarnia Room. Tell him Kira's leaving Allogrenia and has been gone two days.' He thought feverishly. She had exited the Warens through Kenclan before, but Kenclan was north-east, the same direction as the Shargh-lands and he guessed she would choose the Renclan opening instead. 'Tell Penedrin she's leaving through Renclan and that I've gone after her. Penedrin will send scouts to Kest.'

Arlen stared at him, mouth agape and Tresen shook him. 'Go!' he shouted, and waited only to see Arlen flee, before he grabbed his pack and sword and sprinted after him. By the 'green, he hoped his guess about her direction was right!

It would be quickest to go the through the Warens, but he did not know the way well enough and he swerved back down the tunnel towards Nogren. He should have guessed she would leave, he knew Kira best of all.

161

Even Kest had suspected something, but all too late! He pounded through the last cavern, ignored the guarding Protector's exclamation, flung himself past Nogren, and sprinting off again. It was dawn, a small moon still in the sky, not a full one. She *might* be safe. He cursed as he thought of Bern and forced his legs to greater speed.

19

Kira shifted restlessly, making her sleeping-sling jiggle and creak. She felt as if she were the only thing awake in a forest adrowse in the quiet heat of midday. The journey through the Warens had been longer than the map suggested and had taken more time than the journey to the Kenclan octad with Kest.

She had slept on the Warens' hard stone several times, but sleep eluded her now, driven away by roiling thoughts of the Shargh. Why did they hunt her? Was it hatred of her, hatred of healing, or hatred of something else entirely? Why would they hate her anyway when they did not even know her? Yet Kest believed they hunted her, and he was not a fool, and it fitted with everything that had happened.

Her heart raced making sleep even less likely, and she turned over and then back, as the sword jabbed her hip. She did not even know why she had brought it. She was a fool if she thought she could turn into a Terak Kutan and strike her enemies down before they dispatched *her*. The sword-games she had played with Tresen in the Warens had been about stabbing at sawdust-filled effigies, not plunging swords into the flesh and blood of real people.

She concentrated on the lumbering progress of a bark beetle along the bough above as she struggled to still her panic. She wondered what Tresen was doing now, and Miken, and Tenerini. Would they mourn her passing? Her eyes burned, and she swore. Instead of fretting over things she could not change, like the Shargh's murderous ways, she wallowed in self-pity. Not very impressive, *Tremen Leader Kiraon*!

She turned her mind to the strategy that had helped her sleep before and listed the herbal requirements of salves, where the herbs grew, their flowering, the manner of their harvest, of their preparation, of their storage, and had started to drift when twigs snapped. Her eyes flew wide. There were voices!

They were some way off but came in her direction. Her heart pounded but it seemed that everything else in the forest held its breath. Then as the speakers neared, the scattered fragments of speech came together into harsh Shargh words.

How close? How many? Two speakers? Three? They passed to the left of the terrawood and their voices faded leaving Kira shaking. She was barely beyond the Second Eight! What hope did she have of reaching the Third Eight, let alone the forest's border?'

A springleslip fluttered onto the bough above her head, trilled and preened, then darted away through the foliage. The leaves shivered and stilled, then it gave voice again, as springleslips always did. No one knew why they sent a second song. Maybe it celebrated the joy of its flight. Whatever the reason, the springleslips' double song was as much a part of Allogrenia as the song each tree sang, made-up of its unique leaves and twigs and branches.

Kira plucked a sprig of bright new foliage and inhaled its sappy breath. The Tremen left no footprints in the green and growing, but the Shargh trampled and crushed. It made their approach easy to hear, and their retreat easy to track. They were intruders, ignorant and uncaring of the forest's ways, and while her sword might be powerless against them, her knowing was not.

She caressed the sprig of terrawood as her resolve hardened. Allogrenia was worth fighting for, but she would fight as a Healer, as Kasheron intended, not as a Terak Kutan. She must have the Terak Kutans' swords to meet Shargh swords, and would gift the Terak Kutan healing in return, but when it was ended, the Terak Kutan would leave, and the paths the Shargh had gouged would grow over again, the Tremen's wounds heal, and Allogrenia be as it was before.

She took the sword from her belt and pushed it deep into her pack, then hauled herself out of the sling and stowed it too. Her senses tingled, as if she had lost a layer of skin. Hiding in the terrawood wasted time. She would travel through both day and the night until exhaustion ensured she did sleep.

The terrawood trunk was almost warm under her hands as she descended and she paused in its lower boughs to listen. The forest spoke of a breeze, of severs nearby, of tippets and springleslips, honeysprites and flowerthieves, and she dropped to the ground, and briefly placed her palms and forehead against the tree's bole. 'I thank you for your Shelter,' she whispered, and moved quickly away.

Arkendrin tore a strip of smoked ebis fat free and chewed on it as he glowered at the man in front of him. It was some nameless kin of Irdodun's, his face shiny with sweat, his message punctuated by hoarsely drawn breaths.

Arkendrin ground the fat between his teeth as he considered the long and ill-favored day they had endured. They had trawled through the murk with no sightings of treemen but now, as the sultry day turned into a stinking, windy night, the Sky Chiefs smiled on him.

Despite the man's lowly status, the news was good. There was a swift movement of treemen that was different to their usual aimless wanderings. It could only mean something of interest to the treemen was nearby and, as the treemen had never hunted them, it suggested something the treemen wanted to protect.

He had judged rightly to delay, and he swallowed the fat and started on a second strip. The Sky Chiefs had gifted him foresight and now sent the creature to him as a reward for his forbearance. He rose and the air whined as he slashed at the surrounding foliage, then strode to where Irdodun and his kin took their food. 'The Sky Chiefs send treemen this way.'

Some of the Voiceless men laughed uneasily and Orthaken seemed to shrink. 'Maybe they seek *us*, Chief Arkendrin,' he said, his chin shiny with grease. 'Some of the warriors from the lower slope hide themselves as ill as mawkbirds on sorcha roofs.' He nipped at the joint of meat in his hands in quick, nervous bites.

Arkendrin's legs splayed and his hands came to his hips. 'Do you fear them?'

Orthaken blinked. 'I welcome the chance to work my flatsword, Chief Arkendrin, but they provide less sport than wolves. At least wolves have teeth.'

Arkendrin grinned and his gaze shifted to the Shargh to his left. 'Urpalin, do the treemen have teeth?'

'They graze like ebis, so it seems likely.'

Arkendrin threw back his head and laughed, then turned to Irdodun. The warrior was silent as he smeared tesat on his dagger. 'Do your lesser blood-ties speak for you this day, Irdodun?'

'The treemen fought last time, Chief Arkendrin, and they will fight this time. The creature is important to them.'

'And important to us,' said Arkendrin, 'or why else would the Sky Chiefs grant the Last Teller his vision,

166

and my blood its guardianship?' His eyes glittered, and he stabbed at the greenery again. 'The treemen come this way. They intend the creature to see the sun set to seal our doom.'

Urpalin sprang to his feet. 'It won't happen while *I* live, Chief Arkendrin! Not while *I* have a flatsword in my hand!'

Arkendrin's hand slammed down on Urpalin's shoulder and all but buckled his legs. 'It will be the chief's blade that blinds her, and the chief's blade that kills her,' he snarled.

'I . . . I meant only that I would kill those who aid the creature,' stammered Urpalin.

The trees thrashed in a sudden squall of wind and Arkendrin's grip tightened, making Urpalin blanch. 'There will be plenty of killing, even for those of the lower slope,' he said, as his eyes burned into him. He dropped his hand and Urpalin staggered backwards. 'Tesat your flatswords,' growled Arkendrin to those gathered. 'We have work to do.'

Kira stopped in the lee of a castella to pull her cape close against the stinging shower of twigs. The canopy roared and broke to reveal the scud of clouds, and a branch crashed to the ground, making her jump. The night was so thick it was hard to see more than a few paces ahead and the wind's roar obliterated other sounds. The Shargh could be anywhere but there were no stands of bitterberry to hide in, and no terrawoods to climb. Not that she had time to hide if she were to reach the Fourth Eight by dawn.

She took a swig from her waterskin and struggled on. The wind grew but it didn't rain, and she wondered if she caught only the edge of a storm that shed its water elsewhere, or whether it was simply drier in this part of the octad. The ground was certainly hard underfoot and the only annin she had seen was sparse and brown-edged.

She remembered the last time she had been here. It had been spring when bright new shoots had penetrated the leaf-litter, and she had been less than ten seasons old. The journey had taken her more than six days each way, which was a long time for a child, but her father had not reprimanded her or confined her as punishment. He had not cared where she was then, or what she did. He had not cared about her at all—until her healing had rivaled his.

The night had turned before Kira stopped again, and then only to remove something from her boot. She plonked down in a tangle of undergrowth to shake it out, and then sagged back against the bushes, enjoying the brief hiatus out of the wind. The scrubby growths of bitterberry and lissium provided good shelter and she was tempted to stay there, but she put her boot back on and glanced up.

Something was wrong, and her scalp prickled. For some reason she was reminded of the leaves that floated on the Drinkwater. They eddied where the bank curved in or where stone protruded, but in the end, they all went the same way. The shadow she could see seemed odd and she wondered if it were a trick of the light.

The trees bent under the wind and came upright again, so it made sense that shadows ran both ways, but she stayed where she was. The blot of darkness was motionless and that more than anything held her motionless. Then another blot joined it and voices spoke; harsh, disjointed, unmistakable.

They came her way and her heart all but failed her. Now she could see the glimmer of their eyes! Surely they could see hers? They moved inexorably closer, but she could not look away. There seemed a terrible inevitability that they would find her.

Twenty paces, fifteen, ten; their swords and knives were visible, and memories of Kandor's death tore at her mind. There was a crash behind them, as another branch was wrenched from the canopy, and their swords flashed. Then there was another exchange, the words completely alien, and they moved off in the direction she must go.

Kira's hands shook and she struggled to breathe. She should climb a tree and stay there but there were no terrawoods. Maybe a sever would do. The Shargh would not think to look up, then again, the way things crashed down in the wind, they would be fools not to. A ghastly image came to her of Shargh staring up at her sleeping-sling, then soundlessly climbing up to slay her.

What she wanted was a dense stand of bitterberry or shelterbush to crawl into, but the octad was bare of them too. She crept from her hiding place into the next pool of darkness, scanned, and crept on. Her progress was excruciatingly slow, but her fear finally ebbed enough for her to quicken her pace.

The night wore on, but the wind did not ease, and it carried strange, new pungent scents. Kira guessed they came from the lands beyond the trees: the *Dendora Plain*. The understanding she was to leave Allogrenia brought a crushing dread, and she had to force herself to keep going, her back cramping under the weight of a pack bulging with her Healer's kit, nutmeat, dried fruit, and clothes.

The dark faded and she found herself staring up in search of a terrawood to sleep in, but there were only severs and castellas, their leaves silvering in the dawn's first light. The trees were sparser here and she peered about as she walked.

She must be near the Fourth Eight but she could not see any of the darker foliage of an alwaysgreen through the trees. There were plenty of springleslips though, which had quit their rocking roosts early, and whose shrill calls now filled the canopy. Only a springleslip could compete with the wind, she thought dryly, as she watched them dart above her.

She glanced back to the way ahead and her heart stopped. Shargh! She was at least three paces from the shelter of the last sever but to even *move* now risked drawing their attention. There were two of them, but she had no idea whether they were the same two she had seen before.

They were only about twenty paces ahead, busy with their waterskins, but if either glanced around, they would see her. Neither appeared in a hurry, the taller talking and the other nodding at regular intervals. She took a cautious step back, and the speaker fell silent, the listener gave a final nod, and then he half turned.

Terror tore the strength from her limbs, but in the same instant, a figure burst from the trees in front and the Shargh exclaimed and swung back. Kira gasped in horror. It was Tresen, travelling fast, and several paces into the open before he sensed the watchers' eyes.

He spun and drew his sword in the same swift action, then his head lifted fractionally, and Kira knew he had seen her. He hesitated for the briefest of moments, then thrust his sword back into its sheath, turned and fled. The Shargh drew their swords and sped after him.

Tresen! Her wobbly legs meant her first few strides of pursuit were more a stagger than a sprint, but then desperation lent her strength and she raced through the tangle of leaf-litter, roots and broken boughs, her gaze on the backs of the pursuing Shargh. The Shargh were not as fast as Tresen, but their pace was relentless.

The air burst from Kira's lungs in grunts as the land steepened and she scrambled up the slope, using shelterbushes to haul herself forward. Sweat blurred her vision and she clipped a sever and spun sideways onto her knees and, by the time she had clawed way upright again, one of the Shargh had disappeared. Did he run in front or had he looped around to cut Tresen off?

Something launched at her and she ducked instinctively, then the world disintegrated into shouts and screams and the squeal of metal against metal. A hand fastened on her arm and she was wrenched backwards so violently her shoulder muscles screamed, then she was being hauled away back down the slope.

'This way, Leader!'

'Penedrin!' He gripped his sword with one hand and her with the other, as he dragged her away from where Tresen had gone. She clawed at some passing bitterberry and it was ripped stinging through her grip. 'Penedrin, no! Tresen's . . .ahead.' She had no air in her lungs, no air to speak. 'Tresen's . . .'

'Stinking heart-rot!' He thrust her behind him and she landed with a thud and scrabbled her heels in the litter to get clear. Metal clanged as Penedrin's blade thrust towards a Shargh's flesh and was turned aside. They circled each other panting, their sweat acrid on the air, as they clashed. Penedrin's blade found the Shargh's arm and blood sprayed over them both, but the Shargh did not falter and as the fight brought him around, his eyes flicked to hers: black and cold, and full of hatred.

Kira fled back up the slope, reached the top and scanned wildly. She could see two other fights, Protectors darting through the trees, and flashes of movement in the direction Tresen had gone. 'Kira!' She whirled. Kest clambered up the slope towards her, shirt torn, sword brilliant with blood.

Then she heard Tresen scream, low and guttural, and she flung herself down the slope's other side, pelted between the trees and forced her way through a tangle of sour-ripe, slicing her face and hands. Tresen was on his knees, his shoulder laid open from blade to breast, a Shargh standing over him, sword raised high.

The sword started its descent and, as Kira launched herself, the Shargh half turned, snatched the dagger from his belt, and slammed it into her back. The force of the blow knocked her to the ground and blotches of black filled her vision.

Something warm dripped on her cheek as the Shargh raised his sword again. Tresen's blood, she realized numbly. The Shargh's face filled with astonishment and his eyes jerked to a point beyond her, as if he sought someone, then widened in terror. There was the squelch of a sword through flesh, a crunch as it found bone, and a thump as his body hit the ground.

Feet still pounded, and swords still rang, but the sound drew away, like the light, leaving her in quiet darkness. With the last of her strength, she crawled to where Tresen lay. He had fallen backwards, his face turned to the sky. Looking at the trees, she thought dazedly as she collapsed against him. A good way to die.

20

Tarkenda pushed the vent aside and blinked as rain-drops hit her face. The Braghans were eaten by a layer of cloud; the only sign the sun had risen, a silvery glow to the east. The sorcha groaned under the wind, and the billowing roof emptied sloshes of water down the side. The wind had howled like a wolf pack all night and brought a pounding, soaking deluge.

Surely it augured well to finally have rain? The spur was awash, water sheeting down over the slope to the pasture lands below. Was it too much to hope that the grazing would soon be green and the Thanawah's red scum flushed away?

She let the flap fall and came back to the bed. Palansa lay with her eyes closed and her hands clenched on the cover. *Another day*, the birthing-woman had said, and gone back to her sorcha to sleep. Tarkenda remembered all too well the long agony of Erboran's birth, and she settled on the edge of the bed, and smoothed a tendril of hair from Palansa's forehead. At least Palansa had stopped vomiting.

'Do you want to walk again?' she asked.

Palansa's head shook imperceptibly. 'I want it over with.'

'Erboran took two dawns to birth,' said Tarkenda, as she gently stroked Palansa's hair. 'All I wanted was to die. It takes many moons to grow a child, and while he's in your belly, he belongs only to you, and you to him. There's nothing sweeter than that closeness.' She paused. 'I've wondered sometimes whether birthing is so painful because neither mother nor babe wants to let go of the

173

other.' She sighed. 'Men never know that sweetness. Perhaps it is why they're so ready to take their swords to the children of others.'

Tears squeezed from under Palansa's lids. 'I want Erboran.'

'I know,' said Tarkenda.

Palansa moved restlessly and pulled her knees up hard against her belly. 'I want him here with me! Why should I have to do this without him? Why should—' She clenched her teeth and waited for the spasm of pain to pass. 'Why should I have to fight Arkendrin? Why should I have to try and keep . . . the loyalty of those as hollow as slitweed?'

'You're not doing it alone, Palansa, though it might seem so. Erlken sits at the door now, his spear across his knees, as sodden as a newborn ebi unlicked by its mother.' Tarkenda smiled but Palansa's face remained set. 'Squaziseed and shillyflower cakes have been prepared to help you, and in sorchas up and down the spur, Shargh call on the Sky Chiefs to send you strength. Ormadon spends his waking hours plucking whispers from the air and many others use their skills in smaller ways to help protect you.'

Tarkenda hobbled back to the vent. Damp air was no friend to rotting joints. 'It is well that Arkendrin is still deep within the trees. Even if he starts back now, the babe will be snug in its sling before he returns.' She smiled. 'The next chief will be born in peace.'

Palansa's weary face turned to her. 'And afterwards?'

'It is as we've discussed,' said Tarkenda carefully. 'If Arkendrin finds the girl of the Telling and brings her back to kill, many of those now content to wait will join his cause. A chief with fire in his belly and a spear in his hand is always preferable to a babe in his swaddlings.'

174

'Then he will kill my child,' said Palansa thickly, her eyes huge in her pale face.

Tarkenda came back to the bed and closed her roughed hand over Palansa's damp one. 'We are strong, Palansa. We will protect him.'

Palansa gasped and her hand balled in Tarkenda's grip. '*You* are strong,' she said, when she was able. 'I fear everything.'

Tarkenda paused for a moment and listened to the steady tattoo of rain. 'An ebis cow will defend her young against a wolf pack. All we see is one pair of horns against many claws and teeth, but it isn't all there is. The ebis loves its young and love gives it strength.

'When Ergardrin was called home, I despaired as you do now, but I loved Erboran *and* Arkendrin, and that love gave me horns. It defeated the doubters and even the spears of the hollow-hearted.' Her grip on Palansa's hand tightened. 'The babe which struggles to free itself is *my* blood too, and we have horns enough between us to keep him safe.'

Palansa said nothing but her fingers relaxed. 'Now,' said Tarkenda, giving her hand a final pat. 'I will mix you some honeyed water and then you must sleep.'

Something soft and membranous tapped against Kira's face. A bat's wing, she thought nonsensically, and turned away. There was the spicy smell of smoke too and the smell of sweat and blood. The tapping continued, and she opened her gluey eyes to see Kest looming over her.

'I'm sorry to rouse you, Kira, but we have wounded, and we need them up on their feet and away from here.'

Kira raised her head. Her mouth was full of the taste

of sickleseed and her breath caught as appalling memories flooded back. Kest pulled open her sleeping-sheet and eased her up. Every bone in her back felt crushed and she shut her eyes again.

Kest gave her arm a shake. 'We need you, Kira.' His voice seemed far away, and she struggled to focus. 'We've stopped the bleeding, but he must be stitched, and you're the best person to do it, *and* to use the fireweed. We've boiled the stitchweed and made bandages. We've done all we could before we roused you.'

Kira struggled to clear her mind. 'Who?' she mumbled, her voice thickened by the sickleseed.

'Tresen.'

The air stuck in her throat, thick as tree-sap. 'I thought . . . I thought he was dead.' She palmed away tears, powerless to stop them. 'I'm sorry. He's all I've got left.'

Kest pulled her into his arms. 'There are many who love you, Kira. Never think you're not loved.' His voice was ragged then he released her, and when he spoke again, his voice was even. 'Brem doesn't think anything is broken in your back.'

He held up her cape and stuck his fingers through the rent. 'The dagger went straight through this, straight through your pack, and into this.' He produced a shattered pot of bruise-ease, and his weary face broke into a grin. 'Strangely enough, it was the bruise-ease that did you the damage. Apparently, it has the opposite effect to usual when rammed into your back.'

He tossed the pot aside, helped her up, and supported her as she hobbled over to where Tresen lay. She could see no other wounded and she wondered whether they were already dead. 'Others?' she asked reluctantly.

'Two dead. Brem's tended the injuries of the others.'

Tresen was so ashen that even the firelight failed to give him color. She knelt beside him and stifled a groan as pain throbbed through her back. Amazingly, his eyes opened. 'You forgot to say goodbye,' he whispered, panting shallowly, and wincing with every breath.

Kira's eyes burned again. 'Has Brem given you anything for the pain?'

'Sickleseed.' He half raised his head and his pallor increased. 'Not everest . . . Kira. Too dangerous for . . . the Protectors . . . to carry me. We will need to leave . . . at dawn. Shargh are . . . near. I'll put up . . . with . . . the pain.'

'I have to cleanse the wound with fireweed before I can stitch it and you've lost a lot of blood. We both know the shock could kill you.'

'No everest.' He smiled weakly. 'I'm . . . not intending to die. I'm Kashclan remember, as stubborn . . . as you are.'

'We're renowned for it,' she said hoarsely, and coughed to clear her throat. 'I'm just going to check the wound.'

She peeled back the sleeping-sheet and placed her hands over his heart. She had learned from the wounded in the Warens that the pain was strongest there, perhaps because— Her fingers burned and then the wave of fire broke over her and seared her until she thought she could bear no more, then ebbed, leaving her nauseous.

She teetered forward and Kest's strong hands steadied her, careful not to touch her back. He passed her his waterskin and watched her drink. 'Better now?' he asked. Kira nodded.

'It's the strangest thing,' said Tresen. 'The pain is gone.' His gaze moved from Kira to Kest, and back to Kira. 'You took the pain,' he said incredulously, 'but how—'

'She's a *feailner*, like in the Writings,' said Kest proudly. 'A taker of fire. Your clanmate will explain it to you, Protector Tresen,' he said, and moved away.

'How long have you known?' asked Tresen.

Kira unwound the bandages Brem had used to staunch the bleeding. The outer ones were stiff with dried blood, those nearest the wound, sodden. 'Since the first attack, but I didn't understand it then.' She put the bandages aside and reached for the fireweed Brem had set ready.

'So many secrets,' breathed Tresen. 'You didn't tell me you were leaving the Warens either.' Kira said nothing, her attention on the wound. It was deep, but thank the 'green, clean-edged. She picked up the fireweed and Tresen's good hand caught her arm. 'I thought we were friends.'

Kira's eyes flared. 'So did I! Yet you hid from me how Bern died and that it was *me* the Shargh hunted!'

Tresen's grip tightened. 'I was under orders.'

'We're clanmates, Tresen! Doesn't that mean *anything* to you? All the times we spent together, everything we shared.' She jerked her arm free. 'You and me and—' She clamped her mouth shut and lathed the fireweed into the wound.

'It was to keep you safe,' he said hoarsely. 'To keep you from this.'

'There *is* no safety!' she gritted, her eyes on the wound. She took a ragged breath. 'I'm going to stitch this now, and take the pain again, then you must sleep if you want to walk out of here and not be carried.'

Tresen's hands plucked feebly at the sleeping-sheet, his moment of strength spent. 'Don't leave Kira, don't let it end like this.' His words slurred, and his eyes had lost their focus. 'You weren't the only one who loved Kandor.' Kira clenched her teeth, pulled the edges of the wound together, and started to stitch. 'Pledge me you won't leave . . . without saying . . . goodbye,' he whispered, his chest heaving with the effort to speak. She pulled the stitchweed taut and passed the end back through his flesh.

'Pledge me!'

It was a cry and Kira stopped. Tresen's dark brown eyes were fixed on her, though she suspected he could no longer see, and she ran the back of her fingers gently down his cheek. 'I pledge.'

It was close to dark but Kest still stood, sword in hand, in no mood to take to his sleeping-sheet. The burial party had returned without incident, and Bisren and Cadrin now lay in the Fourth Eight's Shelter. The alwaysgreen belonged to Renclan, and the dead had been Barclan and Sherclan but Kest owed the living and it was too great a risk to return the bodies to their own octads.

His jaw set as he considered the custom of burying the dead within the Shelter of their own clan's alwaysgreens. It was one of many Tremen ways the Shargh had destroyed and he had no doubt that they watched and waited, determined to destroy more. He considered the toll of this first clash. His shoulder burned from a dagger score, Penderin had a shallow cut to the hand, and Darmanin a wrenched ankle.

And then there was Tresen, who might not survive, despite Kira's extraordinary skills. Bisren and Cadrin had died, and six Shargh: a better ratio than their first encounter. He grunted. Was this how it was to be from now on? A good day when more Shargh died than Tremen? He wasn't a stinking Terak Kutan! All death was evil, no matter whose.

He sensed rather than saw Nandrin and Jonkesh's patrol around their camp's northern perimeter, and Saresh and Deran's around its southern. The bodies of the fallen Shargh lay in the trees, unclaimed by their comrades, which presumably meant there was not a leader amongst them. Kest frowned as he considered the attack. It had been hard to tell who, if anyone, led it. Two Shargh had clearly been in pursuit of Tresen, but the others had appeared in ones and twos, and in no particular order, probably drawn by the shouts.

The Shargh had blundered about in the undergrowth as if at war with the trees and he had known of their presence before he had seen them, not that the advantage had served him well, not with Tresen running for his life and Kira in the middle of it. Not one of his better leadership moments, he conceded, but then again, no Protector Commander had ever faced what he now did.

Sarkash had trained them to fight in formation, with each man protecting his comrade, not to engage in mad scrambles where they never knew from which direction the next sword blow would come. And at dawn, he would have another sort of fight on his hands, one where he must convince Kira to return to the Warens, and if he failed, to take her there by force.

21

A silvery mist had crept through the trees when Kest woke. He got to his feet and scratched his stubbly jaw. Kira and Tresen still slept, the predawn light illuminating Tresen's deathly countenance, and Kira's weary one. She looked older, the childlike roundness of her face gone, making her look less like Kandor and more like a woman. She lay facing Tresen, her outstretched hand on his arm. *He's all I've got left.*

Kest grimaced. She did not consider him part of her life, despite them being bond-brother and sister, and he could not blame her. Tresen was clan-kin and they had been close since childhood, whereas she had only known him a few moons, most of which he had been fighting her. And now he must fight her again, *and win*, to ensure the Tremen's future.

Kest scratched his jaw again as he recalled the previous occasions he had tried to get her to accompany him to safety. They were not experiences he wanted to repeat and, given her obvious intention to leave, he had no idea how to convince her to return to the Warens of her free will.

He took several paces away from the fire and nodded to Nandrin and Jonkesh as they came off guard duty. Maybe he would argue that Tresen needed her and that, without her aid, his wound would be unlikely to mend.

The trouble was, she knew a lot more about healing than he was ever likely too. Arguing that Allogrenia's women needed her birthing skills, as they surpassed even those of the oldest birth-wives, was similarly flawed. Perhaps— She had woken, and he saw her wince as she

181

struggled from her sleeping-sheet and bent to examine Tresen.

Whatever she found seemed to satisfy her, and she limped over to him. He could tell from her expression she knew she was in for a fight, which was not a surprise, given she was not a fool. 'We must speak, Protector Commander,' she said.

'As you wish, Tremen Leader Kiraon.'

He led her away from the murmured conversations of the waking Protectors, to an ancient castella. Its broad trunk would provide shelter from spears thrown beyond the patrolling guards. He sat down, keen to make the exchange less of a confrontation, and Kira settled beside him, her gaze on the canopy. 'The wind's dropped,' she said in wonder. 'And I've only just noticed.'

'It disappeared as quickly as the Shargh.'

'They haven't gone far.'

'No. Now, Leader—'

Her remarkable eyes fixed on his shoulder. 'You're wounded, Kest. Why didn't you tell me?'

'It will wait. It's only a scratch. Now, I—'

'It won't wait, Kest. Whatever filth the Shargh put on their swords is already working its way into your flesh. Unbutton your shirt.'

'This isn't necessary,' he said in exasperation.

But she had gone back to the fire to reclaim her pack, and he heard the clunk of pots as she returned and rummaged about in it. 'I'm the Healer remember,' she said, setting three small pots on the ground.

'And I'm the Protector,' he said, as he unbuttoned his shirt. 'I'm glad you've reminded me of the distinction, and of my responsibility to protect the Tremen, including you.' She ignored him, her eyes the bright gold he had noticed

182

whenever she healed. He felt the cool touch of the salves first and then the scorch of pain.

'The rot has started and I'm afraid the fireweed will make it worse before it makes it better. I will take the pain before I proceed.'

'I will put up with the discomfort, *Feailner*. I've seen what taking pain does to you.'

'It's part of healing,' she said. She stoppered the pots and grimaced as she stooped to her pack.

'And after you've seen to me, I'll get Brem to salve your back.'

'There's no need.'

'I think there is.' He paused. 'It's part of healing.'

A smile flashed across her face and Kest started, as he glimpsed the beauty he had predicted back when he had first met her. And then it was gone, replaced with the strain that probably clothed his own face.

'I could bandage your shoulder,' she said, 'but it isn't really necessary and might restrict your sword hand.'

'Ah, now you are sounding like a Protector.' It felt like fire coals had sneaked into his shoulder and he struggled not to groan.

'Burning?' she asked.

'Yes.'

'*Fire with flatswords brings the bane, fire without brings life again*,' she quoted. 'The Shargh blades bring a rot that burns and kills, and fireweed brings a burn which cleanses and cures. If I had been quicker in my understanding, many of the wounded would still live.'

'And if I had been quicker learning how to fight, there would have been fewer wounded. It's has been a hard learning for both of us.'

Kira snapped off a frond of castella and turned it over in her hands. 'You should have told me the Shargh hunted me, Kest.'

'Yes. It was a mistake. Miken feared you would throw your life away to save the rest of us, and I agreed. And as it has turned out, he was right.'

'Leaving Allogrenia isn't throwing my life away.'

'The chances of you reaching the Sentinel are small, and of getting beyond it, miniscule. There's more grass than trees near the Sentinels, Kira, and few places to hide. You won't outrun the Shargh either. They aren't fast, but they have great stamina, and the Writings describe them hunting on foot for days.' Kira said nothing but the castella frond was a ragged stem. 'It's safer in Allogrenia,' he finished quietly.

Kira's eyes fired. 'For me, yes, but not for anyone else! I can't live out the rest of my days in the Warens, Kest, and if I go to the longhouses, I will draw the Shargh there. At least if I leave, they will follow me.'

'We don't know that. We know little about the Shargh and less of why they hunt you. And after you're dead, there's nothing to say they will stop their attacks.'

'Is that what you believe?'

Kest hesitated. 'I don't know whether they would be satisfied with your death,' he said slowly. 'What I do know is that I won't allow you to sacrifice your life in the hope that they would. I'm sworn to protect all Tremen, Kira, but the leader most of all. The leader holds the most healing, and healing makes us what we are. My oath is binding and that means I have to take you back.'

She took several paces away and stood in thought, and when she turned, her eyes were a softer gold and her voice calm. 'The Warens don't command the Bough, nor the

Bough the Warens, despite what my father tried to do. You don't have the right *or* the authority to command me to do anything, nor me you.

'Using force against me wouldn't be protection, it would be an attack on the Bough. The Clancouncil would be forced to remove you from command. The Protectors love you and you are the best man to lead them. There would be widespread dissension, perhaps even a schism, and even if the Protectors did bow to the will of the council, your loss would weaken them. Taking me back, *as your prisoner*, would betray those who trust you and compromise the protection of the longhouses. It would be breaking your oath.'

Kest strode to her. He was a good head and shoulders taller, but she did not step back. 'That's an *interesting* idea, Tremen Leader Kiraon, and one, I admit, I hadn't thought of. I give you credit for a *vivid* imagination and *proficiency* with words, but the more likely scenario is this: Kandor's death and Tresen's wounding have unhinged you. Your grief for your younger brother is well known, and it is understandable you might yearn for death for a time. I would be remiss in my duties if I *didn't* bring you back to the Warens, where you might heal and grow strong again.'

Kira's eyes were brighter than the sun. 'I don't yearn for death, *Protector Commander*, I go north to seek aid!'

Kest stared at her in astonishment. 'From the Terak Kutan? The descendants of a people Kasheron broke with because of their brutality? It's unlikely they even remember us, and even if they do, why would they help? Kasheron's parting from his brother was bitter, and I doubt the Northerners have lost sleep since worrying about us since. How many Terak Kutan have visited the Bough to see how we do, Kira? Precisely none.'

185

'They are blood, Kest, and I will go there as Tremen Leader to call upon their leader to honor the blood-link.'

'And how do you intend to get to the north? It's a journey of many, many days,' he snapped.

'I have a map.'

'Oh, and that's going to be *wonderful* protection against spears and swords.'

'Stinking heart-rot, Kest! I am leader and it is my duty to seek help for my people. *Your* duty is to stay here and protect the longhouses. I suggest you concentrate on that!'

'Don't *presume* to tell me what my duty is!' he growled and lifted his hand to remonstrate. Kira flinched and for a moment neither of them moved, then Kest stepped back. Curse Maxen! He was as poor a father as he was a leader. He rubbed his hand through his hair and noticed that his men had ceased any semblance of resting or eating, and openly watched them. He glared at them and there was a hurried aversion of heads.

Then he felt a hand on his arm. 'It isn't you, Kest. I don't fear you.' It was a strange sort of compliment, but he took it as one. 'I've been thinking.'

'That's a good start.'

'If the Shargh believe I'm with you and the patrol, they'll follow you. It will give me time to get ahead of them, even leave the forest before they know I've gone.'

'Why would the Shargh believe you're with the patrol?'

'Well, Nandrin isn't much different to me in height, and if you travelled more at dusk and dawn, and he wore a cape, and checked on Tresen regularly, even walked beside him and seemed to be looking after him, you might trick them.'

'Nandrin doesn't look anything like you and he certainly doesn't walk like you.'

'How do I walk?'

'Not like a man,' he said irritably. He pulled at his hair again. 'You're assuming I'm letting you go.'

'I'm assuming you've accepted that the Warens don't command the Bough.' Kest grunted. 'If you were searching for me in a crowd of Protectors, what would you look for?' she pursued.

'Someone small and finely built,' he answered grudgingly.

'That could be Nandrin.'

'*And* your hair. Nandrin doesn't have a long, fair braid.'

'That's easily solved.' She pulled her herbing sickle from her pack, and before Kest could stop her, severed the braid.

'Kira!' he said, horrified.

She grinned and held it up. 'Now Nandrin will look like me and I will look like an ordinary Protector.' Then her face became serious. 'You will guard Nandrin carefully, won't you?' she asked.

Kest ran his fingers over the heavy silk of the braid. 'Your beautiful hair.'

'Am I so ugly without it?'

The cutting of her hair seemed ominous, as if she were already dead. 'Not ugly, different.' *Like Kandor*.

Her hand touched his arm again. 'Don't be angry, Kest.'

'You can hardly expect me to rejoice in sending you to your death,' he said, as he pushed her hair into his pocket. 'And if you're determined to go ahead with this charade, we had better start now. Pull your hood up and keep your eyes down, and when I address you, put your hands to

187

your sides and straighten your back. If you must speak, deepen your voice, and call me Commander, followed by a respectful bow of the head. I suggest you spend time practising the respectful part; it won't come easily to you.'

Kira fastened her hood, straightened, and dropped her head. She knew Kest's anger stemmed from anxiety, but his manner stirred her own resentments. 'Yes, Commander,' she clipped out, gave a short bow, and strode back to the fire.

22

The men slept with their sleeping-sheets unfastened and their weapons close to their hands. But despite their preparedness for battle, they *did* sleep, unlike Kira who lay wide-eyed, listening to their snores and snuffles. Her fear had grown with the day's ending until the reality of what she intended to do, sat like a stone on her chest that crushed all hope.

No matter how much she castigated herself for being foolish, self-pitying, and cowardly, she came back to the fact that this might be her last night of life. The Protectors would leave at dawn, take Tresen with them, and leave her behind.

She rolled onto her side and combed her fingers through the leaf-litter. If the Shargh killed her in the forest, would she feed the hanawey and frostking, even the mira kiraon before her bones became litter as well? Her hand closed, holding the detritus of leaves entombed, like the earth held Kandor. He was safe from beaks and claws, but did any of it matter once you were dead? Her thoughts were so wild and strange that perhaps she *was* unhinged as Kest had suggested.

It was madness to leave Allogrenia when she had no hope of out-running, out-hiding, or out-witting the Shargh. Maybe she *did* want to be with Kandor but lacked the courage to swallow everest and instead pretended to depart on a heroic trek north. She started as a sleeping-sheet was thwacked down beside her, and Kest settled on it. He eyed her sardonically. 'Not sleeping, Protector Nandrin?' Kira pulled her sheet closer and shook her head.

189

'Does your back pain you?'

'No, Commander.'

'Considering the bruising, I find that hard to believe. I notice you didn't eat with the men. Aren't you hungry?'

'No, Commander.'

'I don't believe that either, and you can drop the *Commander* bit and start acting like a leader.'

'And how should a leader act, Commander?'

'The Bough doesn't command the Warens, nor the Warens the Bough, as you have pointed out, and that makes us partners in protecting the Tremen, which means we work together. So, you can begin your *leaderly behavior* by telling me what is keeping you wakeful when you are clearly exhausted. I might even be able to help.'

She was silent as her fingers dug at the leaf-fall. 'I was thinking,' she said at last.

'Of what?'

There was a long pause and he strained into the darkness, but the fire had burned low, and he could see little of her face. 'Of what happens after death.'

Was she thinking of Kandor, or of herself? Either would be enough to rob her of sleep. 'The Northerners have gods,' he said. 'They believe these gods give them life and take them back at death. The Shargh believe the same. But Kasheron spoke of the dead succoring the living; of seeds sprouting, growing, and decaying to become food for what follows. Even the rains that fall rise again as mist or are sucked back by the summer sun to fall again.'

Her hand gouged at the leaves, building mounds, and flattening them. 'Do you believe what Kasheron believed?' Her voice was dull, her gaze on the litter.

'The proof is all around us.'

She glanced up. 'Do you fear death, Kest?'

190

He took a deep breath. 'I fear the pain which must come with a sword-death,' he said honestly, 'but I don't fear what comes after. When my father died he was very peaceful, as if he'd gone to sleep.'

'A very long sleep,' she murmured, 'with no awakening, never to see the sun rise, or feel the warmth of love.'

By the 'green she was bleak, as if she prepared for her own death. Perhaps he could still persuade her to stay. 'If you came back to the Warens, we could devise a better way for you to go north. If we sent a patrol with you, the Shargh would still know you had gone, but you'd be safer.'

'But the Protectors wouldn't be. A spear through the trees or sword slash would leave them with wounds full of rot and no one to return them to aid. How many times would the Shargh attack before all the Protectors were dead or dying?' She shook her head. 'Enough people have suffered on my behalf already.'

He caught her hand, stilling its violent movements through the litter. 'The fault isn't yours, Kira. *You* aren't to blame for their stinking blood-thirst and *you* don't have to pay for it!'

'But I have to stop it.'

'There's no guarantee—'

Her hand convulsed in his and their fingers locked. 'We've been through this before, Kest. Don't start it again.'

He stared down at her hand and saw again how fine her fingers were. They linked through his in the way lovers held hands. Her short, choppy hair accentuated the planes of her face and he remembered how happy she had been at Turning, her face aglow with love for her brother. If only she were older, more aware, ready to bond, he would court her now, if only to keep her safe.

191

The outline of her slim form was visible beneath the sleeping-sheet and it would be easy to lean over and caress her face, to bring his mouth to hers. He was not new to the art of love-making and even here, surrounded by sleeping men, he was confident he could rouse a passion in her that might turn her from the path she had chosen.

But while Kesilini and Merek had pledged knowing the full gravity and consequences of what they did, Kira knew little beyond healing. And she was Kashclan, who saw the bonding pledge as sacred and who, unlike some of the other clans, remained bound to their bondmates even when the union proved ill.

He gently extricated his hand. 'We will delay our departure for another day,' he said slowly. 'It will help Tresen build his strength. Tomorrow night, when it is fully dark, I will take you to the terrawood grove the patrols report lies to the east. We will take men with us to disguise it as a gathering expedition and you can remain in the terrawoods when we return. We'll make a great show of packing up to leave and depart at dawn. You should remain in the terrawoods until dark. It will be safer to travel at night.'

Kira nodded. 'Another full day of sleep will help Tresen greatly, but he won't be able to journey all day. Will you be able to stop to rest?'

She was careful not to impinge on his role of Commander, noted Kest. How unlike Maxen she was. 'There's no haste to our journey back, in fact, it will be best that we go slowly so you have time to clear the forest while the Shargh follow us.'

Kira swallowed dryly. 'Will they attack?'

'Most likely if they judge our strength to be less than theirs. They've lost six of their number, but time will tell if more have joined them since.'

Kest might speak as if it were a numbers game, but if they hunted her, they would certainly attack, and Kira had to bite back an exhortation to guard Nandrin closely. Kest knew how to look after his men, she reminded herself. 'The Writings are clear on how to treat Shargh wounds and there's a good supply of fireweed in the Warens,' she said hurriedly. 'Arlen and Paterek know how to prepare it and can stitch wounds as well as I can.'

'*No one* can stitch wounds as well as you can, Kira,' said Kest shortly. There was a brief silence. 'Your pack is full of salves and herbs. What are you intending to eat on the journey?'

'I have nutmeat and dried fruit. I've been saving it by eating pitchie seeds and sour-ripe.'

'A Protector needs a double handful of nutmeat to march all day. How much do you carry?'

'I'm smaller than a Protector.'

'One and a half handfuls then and, judging by what I saw of your pack, I'd say you have about five day's supply.'

'About seven days, and I can gather as I go.'

'Really? Have you read in the Writings what gathering is available beyond the trees?'

'No.'

'Neither have I.'

'Kasheron and his followers must have lived on *something* when they came south,' she countered.

'They came on horses and turned them loose when they reached the trees. You can carry a lot more on a horse than you can on your back.' Kira pulled her sheet higher and said nothing. 'I'm not trying to be difficult,' said

Kest. 'As a Protector, I know how much food you need to journey. If you don't eat enough you will lose fat, and then muscle, and you can't afford to lose either. There's no point escaping Shargh blades if you die of weakness and hunger further north. I can give you more nutmeat, but you'll have to leave some of your healing supplies behind.'

'I'm a Healer Kest, I must have them with me.'

'Once you leave the forest there will be no one to heal but yourself, and the best salve for that is food.'

'I always carried my herbal supplies,' said Kira stubbornly.

Kest wriggled slightly to make a dip in the litter for his hip. The sleeping-sheet was pleasantly warm, and his eyelids grew heavy. 'Then compromise and take less of each herb and salve. You might be able to gather more beyond the trees.'

'And where did you read that in the Writings, Protector Commander?'

He grinned. 'Sleep,' he said, and let his eyes close.

Tarkenda fought to control her fear. The bed cover was drenched with birth water and blood, and blackness from the baby's bowels added to the stains. Tarkenda had seen it before when the babe had been lost and its mother too.

The babe should have been born by now! Even *she* had not labored this long. It must be dawn beyond the rain-sodden clouds and it had been a long time since Palansa had even the strength to groan.

The birthing-woman was silent, her hands on Palansa's belly, her head half turned as if she listened. What was there to hear? The wind still screeched like brawling mawkbirds, and still scooped water from the land to dash it back against the sorcha. It was as if the Sky Chiefs vented their fury, that having parched the lands for moons on end, they were now determined to drown it.

They certainly had cause to be angry. Arkendrin had broken Erboran's mourning time *and* plotted to break the line of first-born chiefs, and now, to add to his disrespect, he roamed the forests instead of safeguarding the coming into being of the new chief. Was this the cause of the Sky Chiefs' fury or— Her breath emptied as a terrible possibility occurred to her.

Suppose the Sky Chiefs' *intended* the Telling to unfold, and had bequeathed the Last Teller his vision to *prepare* them for it, not *warn* them of it? And suppose they sent her visions for the same purpose? In striving to prevent her visions from unfolding, it might be *she* who offended the Sky Chiefs, not Arkendrin.

She lowered herself onto a chair. Surely her punishment wouldn't be Palansa and the babe's deaths? She stared at Palansa fearfully. None of her visions had shown Arkendrin as chief which she had taken to mean Palansa had birthed a boy and both had lived, but her visions hadn't shown that either; just fair-haired men on white horses cutting a bloody swathe through Shargh warriors. Why hadn't she thought of these things before? Did the Sky Chiefs gift her a moment of insight, or was she so addled with weariness her mind wandered along strange paths?

'The child's big,' said the birthing-woman, jolting Tarkenda from her thoughts. 'We need to get her up.' Tarkenda looked at Palansa doubtfully. She lay as if dead. 'Take her arm,' ordered the birthing-woman. Tarkenda gripped Palansa's arm and together they hauled her upright. Palansa groaned and her head lolled forward. 'Hold her,' ordered the birthing-woman, and Tarkenda took Palansa's full weight, grunting as her back and hips screamed in pain.

A shudder passed through Palansa's body and the birthing-woman crouched, busy between her legs. Blood dripped off her elbows onto the wolf-skins Erboran had hunted and pooled in crimson puddles. Palansa jerked convulsively and the birthing-woman's heavy frown gave way to a gap-toothed smile. 'Ah, so you have decided to greet the world, have you,' she muttered.

A bloodied fist appeared, perfect in miniature, then a slide of sticky hair and a bluish back, followed by a high-pitched squawk. The birthing-woman blocked her view as Tarkenda struggled to hold Palansa upright and then the food-bag came away.

Tarkenda was aware the birthing-women had cut the cord, but she was taken up with lowering Palansa onto the bed. She pulled the sodden coverings clear and turned back in time to see the birthing-woman don her cape. The sleeping-sling swayed gently, weighted by a small bundle, and Tarkenda fought to steady.

'What is it?' she asked.

'Only a man would give that much trouble,' said the birthing-woman, as she picked up her bag. 'And a chief at that. Keep her abed for the next few days and send for me if the bleeding grows heavier.' She pulled her hood close, turned to the sling and touched her forehead briefly, and then she was gone.

Tarkenda hobbled to the sling and carefully lifted the baby out, then went to the vent and pushed the flap aside. The rain had eased at last and the clouds peeled back to spill silvery light over the Grounds. The babe's dark eyes gazed back into hers and Tarkenda sucked in the watery air. 'Son of my son,' she murmured, and brought her lips to his sticky forehead. The swell of her heart stopped further speech and, forcing her aching back straight, she went to the door and stepped out into the mud.

Ormadon was there in the churn and those who were loyal to Palansa, as well as some of the higher placed blood-ties of those who trailed at Arkendrin's heels. She pulled the swaddlings away and held the babe high. His arms and legs jerked convulsively, and his mouth opened in a long, loud bawl. There was a murmur of approval and Tarkenda gathered him to herself again, wound him snugly into his swaddlings, and ducked back into the sorcha.

Palansa's eyes were open and as her hands fluttered towards her, Tarkenda placed the bundle carefully into her arms. 'Is he well?' whispered Palansa.

'You heard him,' said Tarkenda, smoothing the sweaty hair from Palansa's eyes. 'He is better than you.' She heaved herself onto the bed and turned the bundle towards Palansa so that she could better see his face.

'Erboran's son,' breathed Palansa.

'The son of Chief Erboran, son of Chief Ergardrin, son of all the first-born sons of the Last Teller's Mouth. What will you name him?'

Palansa gazed at him, devouring him with her eyes and Tarkenda smiled, remembering how she had been with Erboran. 'I name him Ersalan.'

'Ersalan,' repeated Tarkenda. Palansa had taken part of Erboran's name as she must but also part of her own as was fitting, for she was now both his mother and father, his carer and protector.

'Chief Ersalan,' said Tarkenda softly. 'You are well-named.'

23

Night had fallen again and the springleslips' songs given way to the frostkings' calls, deep in the trees. It was time. Kira pulled on her pack, adjusted the hood on her cape, and went to where Tresen lay. She knelt beside him. 'Tresen?'

The Protectors sat quietly, taking their evening meal, and Kira was acutely aware of them as she shook Tresen gently. Kest already waited with some of his men on the edge of the camp and she shook Tresen again. She wanted to be alone with him to say a proper goodbye, but Nandrin hovered as any concerned Healer would.

'Tresen?' Her clanmate roused and she waited for his eyes to focus.

'What have you done to your hair,' he whispered.

She tousled it under the hood and made an unsuccessful attempt at a smile. 'It will grow again.' She took his hand. 'I'm leaving now, Tresen.'

Tresen's hand moved feebly in hers, clammy and limp. 'Kest is letting you go?' he croaked.

'He understands I need to leave for the Tremen's sake.'

'He's a fool then.'

Nandrin's breath hissed and she glanced at him worriedly, hoping Tresen's pain would excuse the insult. 'Kest knows we can't defend Allogrenia on our own,' she said quickly. 'I will seek aid from our Northern kin.'

'The Terak Kutan? Let Kest go then.'

'His place is here.'

'*Your* place is here!'

Sweat glistened on his face and Kira extricated her hand. 'I have to go now, Tresen. I'm going to hide in the terrawoods and Nandrin's going to pretend to be me. See? He's already wearing my braid.'

She made another attempt at a smile but Tresen's hollow eyes did not leave her face. 'Your death won't bring Kandor back.'

'I don't intend to die. I intend to bring aid.' The words sounded hollow even to her own ears.

'I love you. Doesn't that mean anything?'

'I have to go now, Tresen,' she said thickly, and kissed him on the cheek. 'May the alwaysgreen Shelter you and guide your way; may its shadow bring you home again, lest you stray.' Her haste robbed the words of meaning and Tresen turned his face away.

Kira got to her feet. Was it to end like this? All their seasons together, everything they had shared? It was probably the last time she would ever see him and yet her mind was empty. She wanted one of the hugs they had shared when she had left him *and* the warmth of the Kashclan longhouse, to trudge back to the Bough, but Nandrin waited. 'Thank you for doing this Protector Nandrin,' she said, touching him briefly on the arm. 'Stay safe.'

'May the alwaysgreen Shelter you, Tremen Leader Kiraon.' He went to bow but caught himself and nodded instead.

Kira made her way to where Kest and the others waited, her cape catching on a sour-ripe vine as she neared them. The small irritation made her feel like sobbing and she was glad the gloom hid her face.

'We walk apart as if gathering,' said Kest briefly.

199

They played a game now, Kira reminded herself. They were Protectors on a night-time forage, and she could not expect Kest to offer her comfort when Shargh eyes might follow their every move. The vine tore her hands as she wrenched her cape free, and she blinked back tears, and followed them into the night.

Irdodun rested his throbbing ankle on a log as his gaze passed over the warriors sprawled in the undergrowth to Arkendrin. He was propped against a tree busy smearing more tesat on his flatsword and daggers. He used his running hand, not his fighting hand, but that was not the only sign of something amiss. While he had said nothing of the wound to his shoulder, neither washing nor binding it, his shirt was stiff with blood and he had slept a good part of the light away.

Chief Arkendrin wounded, Urpalin and five of his lesser kin dead in the rot of leaf and root, but *still* the gold-eyed Healer lived. It was as if the Sky Chiefs smiled on the creature rather than them. A bird broke cover and Irdodun's hand went to his flatsword, and then branches rattled and snapped to the east. He tensed as he wondered whether the treemen had developed an appetite for hunting as well as fighting, but it was only Orthaken returning from scout.

He watched Orthaken stoop low and palm to Arkendrin and strained to hear what Orthaken had learned during his reconnoiter. It was as he expected: having camped with their injured for two days, the treemen prepared to leave.

Twenty of them, Orthaken reported, against their own eleven. Irdodun grunted as he shifted his ankle again in a failed attempt to find relief. Orthaken had miscounted, he concluded sourly, although he would never admit it.

Urmachin had reported twenty-one on his earlier scout. Maybe one of them was off scavenging for the foul things they ate, though the Sky Chiefs only knew what they gathered. He had found nothing worthy of his mouth in his time under the trees.

He rubbed his leg absently as he considered the odds. They had killed two treemen and wounded others, one so badly he had not left his bed since and the healer-creature hovered nearby. He doubted the creature would fight which left eighteen of them, or perhaps seventeen, if Orthaken's boast that he had wounded their chief was to be believed. Irdodun's lip curled. He had seen no sign of it. The man strode about as if he were whole.

Irdodun pushed the crude crutch he had fashioned, deep into the rotting leaves, levered himself up, and hobbled towards Arkendrin. A stinking branch had given way under him as he had run, and he wondered how he was to fight when he could barely walk. He needed to be back at the Grounds.

Arkendrin was on his feet too, his eyes like coals in his pale face, as he slashed at the bushes. 'I'll not lose the creature a third time,' he muttered.

He still used his running hand, noted Irdodun, as he approached cautiously. 'I am wondering, Chief Arkendrin, whether your brother's join-wife has birthed,' he said.

Arkendrin stopped in mid slash and stared at him. 'What matter if she has? A squalling babe is no defence against the evil this creature intends us.'

'You are right, Chief Arkendrin, but its birth would bring offerings and entreaties to the Sky Chiefs. They may have been *distracted* from our cause. It was a great ill-fortune to lose Urpalin and to have the creature slip away *again* when we were so close to ridding ourselves of it.'

'It will be dead by dawn.'

'It would be better to kill the creature at the Grounds. If there is a babe in the highest sorcha, the Chief-mother would have claimed the chiefship for it while we have been away. Those who follow like water down a hill will need to *see* the creature's blood spilled to believe the Sky Chiefs favor you over your brother's seed.'

Arkendrin's eyes bulged. 'I am chief! I need no proof of the killing!'

Irdodun let his shoulders sag. 'It is as you say, Chief Arkendrin.'

There was a brief silence then the unmistakable sound of running feet. Warriors scrambled for their weapons and Irdodun struggled to hold both his crutch and his sword. The thumping grew louder and Urgasen appeared, sweat-stained from his long journey from the Grounds, but showing no weariness in his crisp gesture of honor to Arkendrin.

'I have searched for you these past days, Chief Arkendrin, and give thanks to the Sky Chiefs for your clear trail and the scouts you have seeded amongst the trees. I bring important news from the Grounds: the Chief-wife has birthed a son.'

The warriors muttered but Arkendrin's expression remained unchanged. 'What she has birthed is of no interest to me. The healer-creature is within reach of our swords.'

Urgasen looked at him in surprise. 'The Sky Chiefs' honor requires your return.'

Arkendrin's jaws moved up and down as if chewing ebis fat and the warriors tensed, but Urgasen seemed oblivious. He glanced around and frowned. 'Where are the others?'

Arkendrin's feet had planted wide. 'They fought badly.'

The reply was little more than a snarl and Urgasen paused as he became aware of the silence and seemed to consider his next words more carefully. 'It may be that they fought without the Sky Chiefs' favor, Chief Arkendrin,' he said steadily, 'for those who dwell above have as little liking for the stale closeness of this place as we do. The Sky Chiefs favor the bright openness of the Grounds, for they have sent rain there and a male child to the highest sorcha. For this they should be honored, as we have always honored them.'

'The highest honor will be the shedding of the creature's blood!'

Urgasen stepped back. 'It is as you say, Chief Arkendrin, but I follow the older ways, like my father Urgundin before me. I wish you well in your hunt.' He palmed his forehead again and disappeared back into the trees.

24

Kest hauled on his pack. It was wet with dew and chill against his back. The patrol waited as Athrin stamped out the last of the fire's smolder, and Kest resisted the urge to glance towards the terrawoods as he adjusted his sword. Every one of his Protector instincts railed against what he did and hatred of the Shargh rose like gorge in his throat. 'Yes, we are leaving,' he muttered, under his breath. 'Now you can follow along behind us with your stinking swords and leave Kira in peace.'

He barked an order for his men to come into defensive formation around Darmanin and Tresen. Jonkesh provided an arm for Darmanin, and Brem took most of Tresen's weight, while Nandrin hovered at his other side with his hood drawn close. The heavy dew made the use of hoods necessary, *fortunately*.

Tresen was paler than hoar frost and that he was upright at all was testament to Kira's healing skill. Tresen's wound and Darmanin's ankle made them horribly vulnerable but there was nothing he could do about it. They moved off and Kest snapped off a sprig of silvermint and sucked the dew from its fronds. The pepperminty water sharpened his senses as he considered what might come.

The attack would be sooner rather than later, he predicted, for every step took them closer to their homes and the Shargh further from theirs. If the Shargh followed their usual pattern of behavior, they would head straight for Nandrin. Kest had once thought this denoted a perverse kind of honor but had since realized their desire to kill Kira blinded them to everything else.

The Shargh's single-mindedness made them fearless, but it also made them predictable, and the Protectors could let them pass and attack from behind. Kest had also come to understand that the honor of killing Kira was not to be shared. The Shargh who had wounded Tresen had had ample time to kill her but had hesitated. It was a delay that had cost him his life.

Kest stared around grimly, his men equally stony-faced and their tension palpable. The castellas grew closely here, with ancient trunks that provided them with good shelter from spears but the Shargh with good hiding places. On balance, the trees probably advantaged the Shargh, he concluded. At least the castellas would make the Shargh's running style of attack difficult, unlike the sparser severs ahead.

Somewhere to the left, a tippet chirruped, cut off and chirruped again. Kest's hand went to his sword. Either a hunting bird slid towards the tippet's nest or something else approached. He flexed his shoulder experimentally, the wound burning but thanks to Kira, his muscles loose.

His men knew that Nandrin was in terrible danger whichever way the attack unfolded, as was anyone who got between Nandrin and the Shargh, but the young Protector had accepted the risk with the same good nature as he had accepted the teasing over the braid.

Another shrill piping erupted and Kest jerked his eyes to the trees. If the Shargh discovered Kira was not amongst them now, they would realize the trick and speed back. His heart thundered. Had his advice to remain in the terrawood for the day been a mistake? He shortened his steps to allow Penedrin to draw near and muttered a command, and his orders rippled through the patrol to Tresen, who groaned loudly and allowed his legs to buckle.

Brem called out in alarm and Kest raised his hand to bring his men to a halt. 'We rest here for a time,' he said.

The men exchanged glances, as if they wondered why they had stopped so soon after starting off but formed a defensive circle and removed their packs. Brem spread a sheet for Tresen and helped Nandrin lower him onto it, then made his way to Kest's side. 'You think they're close, Commander?'

Kest nodded and they walked on until they were clear of the guarding men. 'I think they're very close and unlikely to wait much longer.'

Brem stroked his stubbly chin and gazed around as if admired the shafting light. 'And if they discover *our* Healer's a man, they'll go back for the real one?'

Kest nodded. 'I'm beginning to think it was a mistake to tell the leader to stay in the terrawoods for the day. If she'd left at dawn, she'd be well past the Fourth Eight by now.'

'*Or* in their hands. We don't know how many new Shargh have joined them since the last attack, but we *do* know they favor the octad the leader journeys in. No, she is better off in the trees until the battles on the ground are decided.'

Kest was not much comforted by Brem leaving the role of victor open but Brem was right. Just because they had bested the Shargh last time, did not mean they would again. His jaw tightened as he scanned his men's defensive positions.

The Shargh had harried Kasheron and his followers in their journey south, sweeping across the grasslands in murderous surges and then disappearing just as quickly, but it was a style of fighting that had not served them well in the trees. They had probably realized that by now, and he wondered what new tactics they might use. A simultaneous attack on all sides? A wedge driven between Nandrin and his men? He dredged his memory for more of Sarkash's teachings.

'There's fire ahead, Commander!'

Stinking heart-rot! He had his answer! He spun, drawing his sword. 'Maintain defence positions,' he bawled. His men had drawn their swords too, their heads swiveling as plumes of yellow smoke sprang up around them. Were the Shargh intending to burn them out or—

There was a blur, a sickening crunch as something struck him, and then litter in his nostrils as he was sent sprawling. The sword was smashed from his hand and metal squealed as battle erupted behind him.

A Shargh blade swept down and he flung himself over and rolled again as a second slash whistled past, then kicked up with all his strength. There was a crack and a scream as his heel found the Shargh's kneecap, but Kest did not wait to see him hit the ground. He sprinted back towards his men.

And then, to his right, a Shargh burst from the murk. *Leader*, thought Kest; it was stamped all over him. Kest glimpsed Jonkesh launch himself forward and be slashed down, and Penedrin struggle to break free from the fight he was embroiled in.

Then things slowed. He saw the Shargh reach Nandrin, catch him by the throat and drag him upright, and he saw Nandrin's hood come loose and the Shargh's face contort in astonished fury. The Shargh's sword flashed but the stroke went awry as Penedrin, in a final desperate lunge, broke free of his adversaries and plunged his blade into the back of the Shargh's leg.

The Shargh roared and staggered and the nearest Shargh abandoned their attacks, grabbed him under the arms and, with swords slashing, half dragged, half carried him back into the pall. Soon the only sounds were the groans of the wounded and the crackle of the burning forest.

Kira swore under her breath. If she were to travel all night, she should be sleeping now, except sleep was as scarce as winter riddleberries! She glared around at her bower of terrawood boughs. And if she could not sleep *now*, she might as well continue her journey. She had promised Kest to rest during the day, she countered, but there was no rest to be had when her nerves were as taut as saplings under boot-heels.

Curse this waiting! She sat up, making the branch creak, and peered down, but all she saw was more terrawood branches, which of course, was why she had chosen a terrawood to hide in. It must be close to midday. Even given that Kest would stop for Tresen rest, the patrol should be halfway to the Third Eight by now, as should the Shargh who followed them. There was no reason for her to stay here, but she still hesitated.

Kest's instructions to wait for a full day and then travel by night made sense. He had also reminded her that the Shargh saw less well under the trees than the Tremen, especially when the moon was small. Her throat tightened as she recalled his last words. He had asked her whether she still had the owl he had carved for her, and of course she did. It shared its thong with the ring of rulership around her neck.

Let it remind you, Tremen Leader Kiraon, when you are far from us, of your home beneath the trees, and of those here who love you. Kira's hand closed over the delicately carved mira kiraon. The longing to turn back was like an immense unsated hunger and she knew she could delay no longer. Either she must go back, or she must go on.

She stowed her sleeping-sling and descended the tree soundlessly, stopping short of the final boughs to peer out and listen. The forest was still and full of the ripe smells of summer and she leapt nimbly to the ground. She needed to leave Allogrenia and begin the journey north before cowardice took over and she scuttled back to the Warens.

She went on, keeping to the shelter of the larger trees where possible, and came to the Fourth Eight. There were burial mounds between its roots, topped with new-cut turf. *Two dead*, Kest had said after the attack, but she had been too concerned about Tresen to even ask who they were. Stinking heart-rot. She was a Healer *and* the leader. The dead Protectors had mothers, fathers, possibly brothers and sisters, and clan-kin.

She dashed the tears from her eyes and hastened past, scanning continuously as her ears strained for sound. The warmth of the day ebbed, and the chuff beetles' rattle joined the jostle of roosting birds. There were no terrawoods now, but it did not matter, she did not intend to stop. Her shoulders ached from the bulging pack, but fear clothed her like a cape, and she knew that even if she found a suitable tree and set her sleeping-sling, sleep would not come.

There was something else that drove her on too, the knowing that, in the bottom of her pack, lay the pouch of morning-bright seeds. She wanted to reach the Dendora

Plain as quickly as possible or she would be tempted to take one.

A single seed would grant her another day and night of travel before her senses failed her and she would need somewhere safe to sleep. The Warens had provided safety last time, when the morning-bright had finally rendered her senseless, but she was no longer in the Warens and soon, she would not be in Allogrenia either.

The small moon was outshone by the glimmer of stars, but she had never seen the night forest so bright. The canopy had started to break which let in more light and shelterbush and bitterberry grew thickly. Sour-ripe was common too, large tangles of it that formed barriers. In places it even climbed into the trees.

Kira had to detour around each sprawl and then re-orient herself before she continued. She ate its fruit as she went and loaded up every spare space in her pockets and pack. Given the sour-ripe grew here, it should grow on the Dendora Plain too, or so she hoped.

25

Kira trudged on through the night and as the light returned, her astonishment grew. The forest had dwindled, with only severs mixing with slender-trunked and sparsely-canopied fallowoods, and strange grey woody trees with musty-smelling leaves. There were vines she had never seen before too, tangled with the sour-ripe, their red-black fruit crowded with blue-breasted birds despite the day's newness.

Kira had no idea whether the fruit was edible and stopped to pick one, then jumped back as something exploded from the thicket at her feet. There was a flash of white tail and it was gone. Silverjack! She recognized it from the chimes in Kest's room but the word was also familiar from the tales told of the Terak Kutan's lands.

Allogrenia's silverjacks had been hunted when Kasheron and his folk had first entered the forests, and she had always regretted their absence. The Writings told of bright-eyed speed and soft, speckled fur, but no silverjacks meant no wolves, and the Writings told a different, more frightening tale of them. *Be grateful Kiraon, that the mighty Kasheron had the wisdom to rid the forest of wolves*, her father had once pronounced.

There was another rush of movement and Kira started as a second silverjack bounded past. It came from the trees behind her and as the blue-breasted birds fled, the hair on the back of neck shifted. She had not disturbed the second silverjack *or* the birds and then she heard the smash of breaking foliage. She whirled. By the alwaysgreen that Sheltered her! There was *nowhere* to hide!

211

The sound of Shargh voices grew and she dropped to her knees forced a tunnel into the vines. Thorns tore at her, but she burrowed deeper and, as the ground vibrated with thumps, curled into a ball, and pulled her cape over herself. Her heart battered against her ribs, but her clothing was brown and green like the vines and if she stayed absolutely still they might not see her, *unless* they searched for her, *unless* they slashed the thicket with their swords, *unless* . . .

They made a lot of noise and not just in their travel. One of them screamed what sounded like curses and others responded, low and respectful. There were grunts and panting too, as if they strained under a load.

Kira stayed where she was, even after the commotion had faded, too panicked to move. Then new thumpings sounded and she held her breath. The second group lacked the first group's urgency, but still moved quickly, speaking amongst themselves as Protectors did on patrol. Their footsteps receded too but again Kira remained motionless, her face smarting from the scratches and her muscles threatening to cramp.

After a time, chirruping erupted close to her head as the blue-breasted birds returned to their feasting, and Kira cautiously eased back the cape. A jagged row of thorns sat dangerously close to her eyes and she squinted up through the mesh. The new sun burnished the edges of each leaf and made the fruit glow like tree-gems.

She backed out of her self-made tunnel, the thorns tearing her skin and clothes, no more forgiving than on her inward journey. She was ragged now as well as dirty and she had not even left the forest. She sucked the blood from her hand but remained crouched as she strained for sound. The trail of broken growth told her the Shargh had veered east.

They headed home, she concluded, as she recalled the map, then sucked in her breath. The Shargh had left Allogrenia! But only some or all of them? And did that mean they knew she was gone and would stop their attacks?

Her mind raced. The screaming she had heard surely meant they had wounded with them, and that meant they had fought again! By the 'green! How many Tremen had been wounded or killed this time? Nandrin? Tresen? Even Kest himself? She scrambled upright. They would need her! There would be wounds to stitch, fireweed to give, pain to take. She took several quick steps back and stopped. For a moment, the need to go on and the need to go back held her like a moth snared in a stickspider web. The Writings were finished and there were other Healers in Allogrenia. She *had* to go north!

She stumbled on. She was the leader; it was *her* task to call on the blood-link and seek aid from the Terak Kutan! How much nobler it sounded than being a *deserter* who fled north to save her skin! If the Shargh *had* attacked Kest, they would know she was not with the Protectors anymore. If only she knew for sure the Shargh had left Allogrenia for good, she could accept what was to come, even her death. At least *if* the Shargh had wounded, she reasoned that they would not lay in wait for her at the forest's edge.

The day grew older and the pools of sunlight scattered across the forest floor were soon out-numbered the tree-shadows. Flutterwings danced in the clearings, not just the usual green, but pale yellow and gold ones too. The birdsong was different as well.

The blue-breasted birds' light trillings joined those of springleslips, tippets and flowerthieves, and there were other, higher pipings. Kira gazed up at some pale-trunked trees and saw flashes of red brilliant against the foliage, the birds' bright plumage reminding her of the ring of rulership's box of scarlet cloth.

Weariness dragged at her limbs and her thoughts increasingly turned to the morning-bright seeds, but she struggled on, and then, as she felt she could go no further, she smelled an alwaysgreen and the Renclan Sentinel came into view.

She broke into a staggering run and stumbled under its branches, then stood with chest heaving, her forehead pressed against its bole, her arms flung wide to embrace it. The scent of its spicy foliage revived her, and as her breathing steadied, she paced slowly around the tree, her fingers tracing the ridges and runnels of its growth to read its story.

To the north, she could see stands of straggly fallowoods and clearly visible beyond their trunks, a sweep of tussocky grass. So close! The map suggested a greater distance but here it was, scarcely fifty paces away, the Dendora Plain, gateway to the north and to the Terak Kutan, the dealers in death whose swords she must have.

She stepped backwards instinctively, deeper into the alwaysgreen's shade, and then half crouched as a bird winged overhead, dark and heavy, its call as harsh as the Sharghs' voices. All she knew of the world beyond the trees were names on a map, childhood stories of Kasheron's mighty trek and of the Terak Kutan's brutality, and what she saw now.

Every muscle ached with weariness and she knew she must rest or take morning-bright. Summoning the last of her strength, she swung herself up into the alwaysgreen, set her sling where the tree's leaves hid her from the ground, and crawled in.

She had no sensation of going to sleep, so sudden was it, but it was still light when she woke, and she lay for a moment listening. The quiet told her it was the space between the birds of the day finding their roosts, and those of night rousing, and she stowed her sling and climbed back down.

The alwaysgreen's scent reminded her of everything she was about to lose, and she had to force her feet away from its Shelter to the very last of the fallowoods and when she reached it, she had to grip its trunk to stay upright.

The world had been devoured by an immense sweep of sky. It curved up to unimaginable heights and down again to the skin of the earth itself. Here and there trees grew in ones or twos, spare-limbed and scarcely bigger than shelterbushes, but mostly the ground was clad in grass, golden now in the ripe rays of the westering sun.

In the far distance, where the earth met the sky, the land rucked up in mighty ridges. The Azurcades. How was she to cross them? Or the Shelterless plain that stretched before her? There was nowhere to hide, not even tangles of sour-ripe.

Her thoughts turned to the Warens, to its safety, but what she had said to Tresen was true. There *was* no safety.

'One day at the time,' she muttered, and each day of journeying she survived took her closer to the north and closer to the day she could turn her feet for home again. She pushed the tangle of choppy hair from her eyes and stared westward. The sun had started to slip from view, an immense orange ball with its lower half flattened by the earth.

Its rays set the clouds ablaze in crimson and gold and she remained transfixed until the last slice of sun had disappeared, and the fire-laced clouds had dulled to grey. The vast dome of sky washed pink and then darkened to purple, and the vista before her was so empty and yet filled with such splendor that she felt shaken. She had never imagined that a place of no Shelter could be beautiful too.

She made her way back to the Sentinel and sucked in the tree's spicy scent until the world seemed normal again. She knew she should go, but something held her there, and it came to her that she was the first Tremen to ever leave Allogrenia.

It was akin to dying, except there would be no slow procession through the trees, no songs, no one to mourn her as she had mourned no one: not her father, or Merek, or Lern, or—

Without really knowing why, she slipped off her pack and retrieved a cloth-wrapped bundle. Then she knelt and using her herbing sickle, cut out a neat patchwork of sods from between the roots.

The soil was rich and dark, and she used her hands to gouge out a hole and then unwrapped the bundle. For a long moment she simply held it, eyes shut, head bowed, then she gently lay Kandor's pipe in the narrow grave.

'The roots have taken you, the tree grown strong from you, the leaves been spun from you, the wind sung songs of you—' she choked to a stop, scooped up the earth and let it sift through her fingers until the pipe's pale wood was hidden by the fragrant soil. Then she firmed the sods back into place and rose.

Beyond the alwaysgreen, the first stars glimmered in the sky. 'Kashclan thanks Renclan,' she said softly, hefted on her pack, and turned northwards.

216

Tarkenda leaned back against the sorcha. The last of the sunlight reflected off the hide behind her and she reveled in its warmth. It brought ease to her aching joints and Palansa and the babe brought ease to her heart.

They sat beside her, Palansa holding the babe close as he suckled. His tiny fists pummeled her breast and he made small, satisfied grunts. Palansa's eyes were locked to his as she caressed his pink wrinkled feet and Tarkenda smiled at his sounds of pleasure. 'You are missing the sunset,' she chastised.

'They will be plenty more,' said Palansa, not looking up.

The clouds blazed red and then, as the earth ate the sun, the warmth began to ebb. Bessel moths fluttered past Tarkenda's face, and she rose and stretched.

Palansa rose too, the babe nestled against her shoulder, his face dreamy with milk. She rubbed his back absently, eliciting a bubbly burp, and ducked back into the sorcha.

Tarkenda lingered, her gaze moving from the Grounds to the Braghans, purpling now like the sky, to the Cashgars clustered at the mountains' feet, and its cave.

There the Sky Chiefs had bequeathed the Last Telling, and the Last Teller had made Ordorin his mouth, seeding the line that had given her a join-husband, a Chief-son, and now Palansa's suckling. What else would come of it only time would tell.

End of The Kira Chronicles series: Book 2 The Silence of Stone

Continue Kira's story in Book 3 The Secrets of Stars or enjoy the whole series in a single book: The Kira Chronicles – Complete 6 Book Series

Take a peek at Book 3

Caledon stopped and turned. 'Why do you delay?'

Kira's heart thundered and she glanced around at the wooded slope. He would catch her if she ran. His build suggested speed and he knew these lands, while she knew nothing *except* he had lied.

'Why do you delay?' he repeated, in Terak this time.

'We're going west,' said Kira in Tremen. 'You *told* me you were going north. I agreed to travel with you because you were going north. You lied to me.'

'Until we cleared the Pass, we *were* going north.'

'But we're not now!'

He came back and she braced herself, but he stopped several paces away. 'I'm taking you west to my friends in Maraschin,' he said evenly. 'We need to rest and replenish our food before we journey north.'

'I'm not going to Maraschin!'

'It's twelve days from here to the northern city of Sarnia, and to reach it, you must traverse the Sarsalin Plain. Without my food, what are you going to eat, Kira?'

'What I stinking-well ate before I met you!' By the 'green! What a gullible fool she had been!

'I would gift you *all* my food for the sake of our friendship,' he said hurriedly, 'but even that wouldn't be enough. You would starve to death before you reached Sarnia or fall victim to wolves. I have friends in Maraschin,' he repeated. 'We can restock our food supplies and go on together.'

'I'm not going *anywhere* with you!' she all but shrieked, then gasped in horror as movement caught her eye.

Caledon spun and drew his sword but there were men all around them, wood creaking as bows were bent and barbed arrows aimed at their hearts. There was a tingling hiatus and then Kira was seized from behind and felt the cold metal of a blade against her throat.

An order was screamed in Onespeak. 'Drop your sword or we will kill her!'

I hope you enjoyed *The Silence of Stone Book 2 in The Kira Chronicles Series.* **Authors need reviews!** It is how our readers find us. I would love you to leave me an honest review on Amazon, Goodreads, or another of your favourite reader sites. Read on to discover my other books.

Works by K S Nikakis
Available on Amazon KDP and a range of digital platforms.

Non Fiction

Journey: Seeking the Sacred, Spirit and Soul in the Australian Wilderness

When we set out into the wilderness, what is it we *really* seek?

Do we seek new sights or do we seek new selves? And are we *really* on one journey or on two?

Journeying fifteen thousand kilometres into Australia's blood-red heart, Nikakis discovers that every journey is perilous, for travellers risk carrying the clutter of their outer lives with them; a clutter that blinds them to the other journey they crave; that of the inner *soul-journey* into a deeper understanding of self.

To enter Australia's vast Outback wilderness, is to enter a place of endless horizons; a place doused with brilliant gold dawns and dazzling sunsets; a place silvered by star-encrusted night skies and, most importantly, a place of hidden sacred places in whose deep stillness our inner

220

journeys can at last unfold.

In the spirit of travellers like Robert Macfarlane and Scott Stillman, Nikakis asks what it is we really see, feel and understand when we follow in the steps of those who have gone before us deep into the wilderness.

Drawing on her Ph.D. in Joseph Campbell's hero myth, and using original poetry and novel extracts, Nikakis takes us on this second journey; a journey of the sacred, spirit and soul, where our inner selves finally have the time and space to gift us richer and more fully-realised lives.

Fantasy Novel Series

Angel Caste 5 Book Series – available complete in one book or as five individual books: Angel Blood, Angel Breath, Angel Bone, Angel Bound, Angel Blessed.

Angel Caste – Complete 5 Book Series - *A modern female hero on a timeless quest*

A troubled half-angel, a beautiful angel guide, a binding promise . . .

Viv is on day release from jail to attend the funeral of the thug she thinks is her father, when she comes face to face with her real father, the powerful angel Archae Kald. If finding out she's a half-angel isn't shocking enough, Viv discovers her mother isn't dead after all but lost somewhere in the tangle of worlds called the Rynth.

Determined to find the only person who has ever truly loved her, Viv goes to Kald's angel world where he appoints the beautiful Thris as her guide. Thris is kind and caring, unlike the males Viv has known before, but after living on the streets, Viv finds it almost impossible to trust.

Friendship grows as Thris trains her to travel the rifts, but the Rynth is a dark and dangerous place, even for angels and, as Thris grows increasingly tempted by Viv's emerging angel traits, disaster strikes.

Viv journeys on alone and stumbles into a war zone where she finds a lost child. She pledges to take the child to safety but, as the war rages on, deciding who is friend and who is enemy becomes a deadly game of chance.

Bound by his promise to guide Viv to her mother, Thris embarks on a desperate search for her, but a greater threat confronts them both and, in the end, they must fight not just for their own lives, but for the lives of those they love.

The Kira Chronicles - 6 Book Series – available complete in one book or as six individual books: The Whisper of Leaves, The Silence of Stone, The Secrets of Stars, The Thunder of Hoofs, The Crying of Birds, The Music of Home.

The Kira Chronicles – Complete 6 Book Series – *traditional fantasy with deep forests and high stakes*

A gold-eyed Healer, a prophecy, two brothers at war.

In seasons long past, twin gold-eyed princes sundered a kingdom. Rejecting his brother Terak's warrior ways, Kasheron led his people deep into the great southern forests and established the healing settlement of Allogrenia. The Tremen flourished, upholding Kasheron's legacy of peace and healing, and protected by the vast, trackless trees.

All Tremen delight in the healing arts, but Kira is the greatest Healer of them all.

To the north of Allogrenia, drought ravages the Shargh's land, and as their suffering escalates, the chief's younger brother seizes on an ancient prophecy to snatch the chiefship for himself. The prophecy links the Shargh's doom to a gold-eyed Healer, and Kira has gold eyes.

The Shargh attack with devastating consequences and Kira must fight to save the wounded, but the Shargh wounds rot, no matter her skill, and Kira finds herself in a deadly race against time. As the slaughter continues, she makes the horrifying discovery that the Shargh hunt *her*. To halt the attacks and save her people, she sets off for the North to seek aid from her long sundered warrior kin.

But the dangers beyond the forests exceed even the Shargh attacks. The Tremen detest their warrior kin but Terak's descendants have inflicted a worse fate on the Tremen. Kira's new-found love is torn apart by ancient hostilities and when trust turns to betrayal, it risks everything she fought for.

As the battles rage on, Kira becomes increasingly sickened by the bloodshed. Desperate to end the suffering once and for all, she sets out on a quest that could cost her everything and everyone she loves.

Fantasy Novels

The Emerald Serpent – *the Celtic Fae in a fight for survival*
Book trailer: https://www.youtube.com/watch?v=bGpKxnpCEMg

Betrayal, torture, death: Etaine lives on only to destroy those who robbed her of everything she loved.

Seven years before, Etaine met fellow Ranger Cormac, the he-Eadar she believed was her longed-for true-mate. Emerald-eyed, white-skinned, and black-haired, the Eadar had formed into Ranger bands to fight the Fada, invading religious zealots determined to replace the Eadar's Serpent Goddess with their own gods of stone.

The pure blood of the ancient Eadar runs strong in Etaine and Cormac's veins, and their joining had the potential to open the Emerald and Serpent Ways to them, old worlds only true Eadar can enter. But their love affair goes tragically amiss, with catastrophic consequences.

Etaine flees and as the years pass, slowly rebuilds her life, but the Fada's attacks grow more ferocious, and the Eadar are forced to fight for their very existence. When the Fada mass to commit yet more bloody slaughter, and the bands join in a final, desperate effort to defeat them, Etaine comes under Cormac's command, the very last Eadar she ever wants to see again.

Together they have a weapon that can destroy the Fada, but to use it, Etaine must learn to trust again and Cormac to Remember. And time runs short: the Serpent rises.

Heart Hunter – *a female hunter on an impossible quest*

Fleet is a young Sceadu hunter: skilled, strong, and fast. She hunts deep into the icy mountains, seeking meat for her people, for the rains have failed and plunged the Sceaudu into hunger.

Her hunts are hard, but she has much to look forward to. Soon she will be gifted her air-name by the Sceadu's shaman, and then she will be a full adult, and free to marry the man she loves.

But while Fleet is on hunt, the old shaman dies, and the new shaman visions a very different future for her: cross the frozen, ice-locked mountains and complete a perilous quest or lose the man she loves forever.

In a moment of anger and frustration, Fleet commits a terrible wrong and sets out into the frigid mountains to atone with her life. In a journey that takes her deep into the earth's darkest places, into strange new worlds, and even into Death itself, she discovers that only she can save her people. To survive, she must draw on every shred of her hunter strength, and doing the impossible, it turns out, is just the beginning.

The Third Moon – *science fantasy with a very human quest*

Where does the past end and the future begin?

Haunted by inherited memories of his people's dispossession and theft of their children, Warrain is just twelve years old when the nightmare repeats. But Warrain isn't living on Earth in the 21st Century, he is living on the planet Imago in the far flung future.

Five years before, Station One's Mech's got high on the opioid arrash, and in the bloodshed that followed, Warrain's scientific community were expelled from the Station, his father murdered, and his mother and unborn sibling lost to him.

The scientists carve out a rudimentary Station high in Imago's ranges, and Warrain's friends get on with their lives. Not Warrain; he climbs the Tors to stare down at Station One, dream of his mother and sibling, and plot revenge.

And then one day, everything changes. A third moon appears in the sky, one of Imago's life-forms calls him by name, and disease breaks out at Station One.

When the Mechs visit to seek help for their ill, Warrain seizes the opportunity to deal them a blow they will never forget. But the third moon brings changes that threaten them all and, to aid the life-form whose kind is being dispossessed and slaughtered, he must turn his back on the hate that has long sustained him and find another way to live.

Messenger – *a dystopic future filled with hope*

In a world made deaf by hatred, who will hear the messenger?

Severine's world ends the day her family is murdered. Being raised in the loving community of gay Travelers always marked her as an outsider, but being female puts her in mortal danger. Women are scarce, precious, and hunted.

When chance brings Severine face to face with the father she has never known, he assigns the son of his murdered best friend to guard her. They soon clash. Severine believes all men are violent brutes and Jeph resents his freedoms being curtailed.

An uneasy understanding grows but Jeph is glad to deliver her to the Enclaves, a sanctuary her father has carved out in the mountains for his women and children. But there is no safety in a world broken by war and sickness and when violence follows her, Severine flees to the northern city of Andhaka in search of a home amongst her mother's people. Jeph follows, bound by loyalty to her father, but the north holds terrible dangers for him.

It's been years since Andhaka has welcomed outsiders with anything but bullets, and to survive and to protect Jeph, Severine must learn to use her enemies' weapons against them. As the stakes rise, she comes to understand the horror of her mother's loss, and what drove her father north seventeen years before. His quest becomes her quest, but she hasn't counted on the savage legacy that war and sickness have left behind, or on falling in love.

I Heard the Wolf Call My Name – *gender-fluid shifters in search of home*

Finalist Best YA Novel – 2019 Aurealis Awards

Jax is just twelve years old and in bird-form high above his island home, when it explodes, killing everyone on it. He believes he is the only survivor until ten years later, he comes face to face with his boyhood friend, Matiu.

Matiu is military and the military need shifters for a crucial mission, but Jax refuses. Having spent ten long years burying his bizarre shifter past, he isn't about to resurrect it. But Matiu rouses other feelings too that Jax finds harder to ignore.

As the military ramps up pressure to force Jax's cooperation, he shifts to bird-form and flees to the last remaining island where he crash lands in the middle of Anahera's vision-quest. She searches for her skin-spirit animal to transform her into a protector of her people, and dreams of finding the white-wolf, but finds Jax instead. To save him she must abandon her quest but her kindness only adds to Jax's turmoil.

To decide who he truly is and where he really belongs, he must first confront his painful past, but that isn't the worst of his problems. The forces that blew Jax's island out of existence now threaten Anahera's as well, and he might just be the only shifter who can save it.
And time is running out.

Fantasy Short Stories

The Gift – A Deep Fantasy Short Story #1 – free on my website at www.ksnikakis.com

Excerpt:

Thariel sat for a long time, surveying all around her, as if she ate the world that would soon be memory. Then she took the harness from the mare, and with soft words, thanked her and bade her farewell. Her own feet she turned towards the forest, tossing her face-plate aside as she went, so that her hair fell loose to her waist, then she discarded her chest-armour, the sword and dagger, her bow and quiver.

The trees closed in and she came at last to the lake Men call Menios and stood for a while on its shore. An owl cried and a mouse shrieked, and all around her the souls of the newly dead jostled in their journey to the void. She stepped into the water and the new life inside her quivered.

'Fear not, little one,' she whispered, in her own tongue. 'We are going home.'

The Tale of Prince Anura – A Deep Fantasy Short Story #2 – free on my website at www.ksnikakis.com

Excerpt:

I should have been happy, for she was beautiful. Dark rivers of curls, skin as white as moonlight on water, breasts softer than spawn, and she loved me well. But her chamber was small, no matter the comfort of her bed, and the old feelings of entrapment rose, as persistent as gas that bubbles from rot below still waters.

I sat at the casement and listened, as I had once loitered near the watery skin of the second world and waited. The moon grew large and small many times, but it came at last, as I knew it would. The soft lament on the night-time air, the song of a soul as confined as mine. It took me a journey of many days through the depths of a massive forest to find her tower.

Stone it was and sheer, and as remote as the third world's glimmer had once been. I sang to her and she answered with sweet melodies of her own and we made love as frogs do, with our voices. And when trust had built, she let down her shining ladder of golden hair.

Glass-Heart – A Deep Fantasy Short Story #3

Finalist Best YA Short Story, Aurealis Awards, 2019.

Excerpt:

Geth moved amongst his band, exchanging quiet words while they waited. Some he had fought with since the Tallon's foul ships had first found their shores while others had come later, when the burn of cot and kin had sent them from their valleys.

Hate drove them but hate was no shield against arrow and knife. It was fighting skills that kept them hale, and Geth ensured they had them aplenty. He needed them living, not just for their own sakes and his, but for what would come later. When the Tallon's stain had been scoured away, the destroyed must be rebuilt.

Kyth sat alone and he went to her and gazed about. 'The glass-heart's fled, has it?'

'I sent her to a place of safety. She will come to me when it is over.'

'Safety was what I wanted for you!'

'And what I wanted for Nyar.' Her eyes caught the star-sheen as she looked up at him. 'But you can't always have what you want, can you, Ceannasai?'

Dragon Sprite – A Deep Fantasy Short Story #4

Excerpt:

Genn rocketed straight upwards, not just because she enjoyed seeing the limitless blue sky before her, but because a Waiwin's wing shape made vertical flight harder for them. Orin didn't try to catch her but swept in circles around her, gaining height in an ever-narrowing spiral. It was a clever tactic and one Genn didn't believe he had thought of in the instant she had cleared the trees. He had obviously studied her strategies and developed a plan to counter them *or so he thought*.

Genn waited until the spiral narrowed to *axeel*, the minimum distance a Waiwin must keep from a Velven unless she *accepted* him, then swerved towards him, narrowing the distance between them. Orin's eyes flashed to black, shocked she *had* accepted him, but before he could act, she folded her wings and dropped.

The strength that had driven Orin's pursuit had surged to his wing-tendrils in anticipation of locking them with hers and he would struggle even to stay airborne until it flowed back.